Discoveries in the Shriver Family Attic

How a Woman and Her Children Dealt with the Battle of Gettysburg

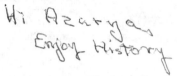

Kajsa C. Cook

Kajsa C. Cook

December, 2014

WHITE MANE KIDS
SHIPPENSBURG, PENNSYLVANIA

Unless otherwise noted, the illustrations are by the author.

This book is a work of historical fiction. Some names, characters, places, and incidents are products of the author's imagination and are based on actual events.

The acid-free paper used in this book meets the guidelines for permanence and durability of the Committee on Production Guidelines for Book Longevity of the Council on Library Resources.

For a complete list of available publications
please write
White Mane Kids
Division of White Mane Publishing Company, Inc.
P.O. Box 708
Shippensburg, PA 17257-0708 USA

Library of Congress Cataloging-in-Publication Data

Cook, Kajsa C.
   Discoveries in the Shriver family attic : how a woman and her children dealt with the Battle of Gettysburg / Kajsa C. Cook.
       p. cm.
   Summary: In the summer of 1867, as they and their new friends explore the attic of Sadie and Mollie's home in Gettysburg, Sadie and her family share their memories of the difficult times during the war.
   ISBN-13: 978-1-57249-398-8 (pbk. : alk. paper)
   ISBN-10: 1-57249-398-4 (pbk. : alk. paper)
   1. Gettysburg, Battle of, Gettysburg, Pa., 1863--Juvenile fiction. [1. Gettysburg, Battle of, Gettysburg, Pa., 1863--Fiction. 2. United States--History--Civil War, 1861-1865--Fiction. 3. Memory--Fiction. 4. Friendship--Fiction.] I. Title.
   PZ7.C769835Di 2009
   [Fic]—dc22

                                                                    2009005149

PRINTED IN THE UNITED STATES OF AMERICA

Contents

Acknowledgments

Thanks to Nancie and Del Gudmestad for their dedication and hard work in restoring the Shriver House and researching information about the family. They gave me the opportunity to serve as a tour guide. Because I spent so much time in the Shriver Museum, I felt that I knew the family and was compelled to write this story.

Thanks to Tillie Pierce's diary*, for without Tillie's memoirs we would never have known what happened during those frightening days of the battle.

Thanks to William G. Williams, author of *Days of Darkness: The Gettysburg Civilians,* for his valuable suggestions and generous help in verifying historical facts.

I thank my family and friends for encouraging me, especially my son Jeff, his wife Nancy, and my grandson Chad. Without Chad's help I couldn't have used a computer and would have had to resort to pen and ink!

---

* *At Gettysburg, Or What a Girl Saw and Heard of the Battle.* A True Narrative by Mrs. Tillie Pierce Alleman. West Lake Borland, New York, 1889.

Prologue

Throughout history, wars have caused so much suffering, not only to the men who fought so valiantly, but to all their loved ones. This story could be a story of any war and its effect on everyone involved.

The Civil War was over in 1865, almost two years after that fateful, never-to-be-forgotten battle at Gettysburg that caused vast destruction to the farms and countryside. By 1867, the town of Gettysburg, Pennsylvania, had almost returned to normal. Fences and homes had been replaced; farmlands and orchards were flourishing; yet, whether the people who lived in Gettysburg and suffered through the battle were back to normal was another question.

Discoveries in the Shriver Family Attic is inspired by the lives and experiences of the Shrivers, a real family who lived on Baltimore Street from 1860 until 1865. The Shriver family name has been documented both as "Shriver" and "Schriver." The "Shriver" spelling was chosen in this story to correspond with the majority of the documents on the family that can be found at the Historical Society of Adams County, Pennsylvania. The story is based on facts, and all characters are based on real people who actually lived in Gettysburg with the exception of Jason and Amy, who are fictional characters.

The Shriver House

To the right is the Pierce house. The Garlach house was to the left of the Shrivers' home.

Chapter 1
Spring 1867

Sadie hadn't minded hanging the wash on the clothesline or feeding the chickens or collecting the eggs with her sister Mollie's help or even lugging five buckets of water from the pump out to the kitchen. Mama could use all the help she could get, having the newborn baby in the house. Sadie and Mollie hadn't realized how much care a baby needed, or how much extra washing one made! Until now Mollie had been the baby in the house, so to speak. But Mollie was almost ten and quickly becoming a big help to her mother and older sister since the arrival of their baby sister, Lillie. Mollie did not remember the baby their mother and father had when she was almost two. He only lived a few months. Sadie slightly remembered him and hoped that nothing would happen to her new baby sister.

In the afternoon Mama planned to bake and Mollie was going to help. Mollie loved to help with baking and cooking. Sadie never minded doing the chores, but she didn't like working in the kitchen. Since Mollie did, she hoped to persuade Mama to let her go for a walk. It had been a hard winter. The snow had finally melted, but now the roads were so sloppy that shoes were covered with mud. It was a beautiful spring

Saturday, warm and sunny. The trees had clusters of pale green leaves, and the birds were busy building nests. Daffodils and tulips were in full bloom. After an extra cold winter, Sadie was restless. She wanted to go for a walk and, well, just think.

"Mama, I did everything you wanted this morning. Mollie wants to help you bake, so can I go for a walk? It's so nice today. Please?"

"If you take this letter to the post office and then invite Mrs. Pierce and Mrs. Garlach to come for tea tomorrow, you can take a walk," said Mama. "Now that you're almost twelve, you'll probably want to take lots of walks. Maybe some boys will be asking you to take a walk with them. You know that means you like each other," teased Mama.

"Oh no, I don't want to walk with any boy," said Sadie, shaking her head. She grabbed the letter before Mama could change her mind and skipped out the door.

She decided to go to the post office first and then visit the Pierces and the Garlachs. As she ambled down the road, she kicked at every stone in her way. It was very satisfying to see the pebbles roll and bounce to the other side of the road. She sighed. Life was so different now. First Papa had died in the war! Then Mama sold their home when the war was over and they went to live with Grandpa and Grandma Weikert on their Taneytown Road farm about three miles southeast of Gettysburg. While there, they helped care for the animals and helped Grandma with the canning of fruits and vegetables—and of course helped in the fields and the garden. Both she and Mollie loved to tend to the newborn lambs.

Little Round Top, the site of the battle's second day, was practically in the farm's backyard. Sadie knew she would never forget those terrifying days. She knew many men had been killed or wounded because she had heard their moans and screams. Mama had sent her and Mollie upstairs to Grandma's bedroom so they would be as far as possible from all the horror and violence. She remembered covering her ears and shutting her eyes while tears streamed down her face. And finally she heard Mama running up the steps and, seeing her daughters huddled in the corner, had put her arms around them. She had never been so glad to see her mama. Mollie had sobbed while she told Mama how scared they were.

She was so immersed in her thinking that she was surprised to find herself in front of the Pierce house. And there was her old house next door. Well, it wasn't where she lived anymore, but it would have been so wonderful if Papa was still alive and they would still live there. But now Mama was married to Mr. Pittenturf and they lived in his house on High Street, only two blocks away, with the new baby.

"Hello there, Sadie." Mr. Pierce was digging in his garden. He leaned on his hoe, smiled and said softly: "My, you are sure growing up. Pretty soon you'll be a young lady. We haven't seen you since you moved back to town. Come set a spell and tell me how your mama's doing, and how is Mr. Pittenturf? Guess it seems strange to live in a different house and have a new father and another sister. I know Daniel

Pittenturf. He's a fine man. A bit quiet, but steady and a hard worker. He'll make your mama a good husband and take care of your family well. You know, Sadie, your papa would be glad to know that someone is taking care of you."

Sadie sat down on the old weathered bench on the edge of the garden.

"I miss Papa. It's not the same now." Sadie bent her head so Mr. Pierce couldn't see her tears.

He patted her shoulder. He knew she was feeling the loss of her papa.

"By the way, Sadie, Tillie wants you to come see her and bring Mollie. She'll be home tomorrow. She went to see relatives in Greencastle. That is a long trip, having to ride over that mountain. She got a ride with the Warner family. Hope that wagon of theirs will make it up that mountain or everyone will have to get out and push. Their two horses aren't too young."

Sadie imagined Tillie pushing that wagon up the mountain in her next to best dress and had to grin. Tillie was tall and slender and always looked so elegant, but, no doubt, if she did have to help push the wagon, her hair would come undone, she'd be sweaty and not happy at all.

"Well, Mr. Pierce, I hope the horses didn't need any help!"

"I hope so, too. Hard to imagine Tillie getting all hot and dusty. After all, she learned to be a lady when she attended Eyster's Seminary School for Girls. Now that she is nineteen and has a beau, I doubt she would want anyone to see her looking a mess."

Sadie liked Mr. Pierce. He had been so good to their family when Papa had joined Cole's Cavalry in Maryland. The Pierces worried about Mama left alone with two small girls. It was hard not having Papa there. The Pierces and the Garlachs helped as much as they could.

"I'm glad I saw you, Mr. Pierce, but I'm supposed to invite Mrs. Pierce to tea. Mama said to invite Mrs. Garlach, too."

"Well, you can kill two birds with one stone, Sadie. Mrs. Pierce is over at Mrs. Garlach's and no doubt yakking away. You know Mrs. Garlach and how she loves to talk, on and on and on. I don't know how she keeps on talking without taking a breath. It's amazing. Oh, by the way, your old house is empty. The people who bought it from your mama moved to Ohio. Maybe they thought it was haunted! You know, because of what happened there during the battle."

"Thank you, Mr. Pierce, I'll tell Mama the house is empty."

Sadie hurried across the yard where she had lived. She felt sad to see how the garden that had produced so many wonderful vegetables now was overgrown with weeds. They had always canned enough vegetables to last all winter. Most of all she remembered all the weeds she had pulled. Mollie would collect them and pile them on the edge of the garden. Mama had started a garden at their new home after Mr. Pittenturf had dug up the soil, and Sadie knew that soon there would be more weeds to pull.

She saw the two ladies sitting on the Garlachs' back porch just as Mrs. Pierce called to her, " Sadie, my dear, what a nice surprise."

Mrs. Garlach waved and then disappeared into the house. Soon the screen door opened with Mrs. Garlach holding a basket. "Sadie, this is for your mama. I made a pie and there are cookies in here too."

"Thank you kindly, Mrs. Garlach. Mama will be pleased. Oh, and she invites you both for tea tomorrow afternoon."

"Why, we'd love to come. Mrs. Pierce, you can go, can't you? We'll enjoy seeing your new home and we can't wait to hold that beautiful baby! Tell your mama we'll be there around three o'clock."

Hastily, Mrs. Pierce arose and turned to Mrs. Garlach. "Yes, we'll be there, but Sadie better leave, or her mama will wonder where she is. So off you go, Sadie, and we'll see you tomorrow."

With a wave, Sadie scurried through the backyards. She was anxious to tell her mama that their old home was empty. She mentally walked through the rooms. A wide center hall divided the kitchen and sitting room from the parlor. Upstairs were four airy bedrooms and above them was the garret or attic. Sadie recalled how she and Mollie used to sneak up there and play dress-up with some of Mama's hats and dresses amid the mysterious trunks, boxes, and old furniture.

The house also had a cellar that Papa had made into a saloon. He had also built a ball alley out back.

The Shrivers had moved to Gettysburg when Sadie was five and Mollie was three. How proud Papa was to put his family into this beautiful home. He and Henrietta (Hettie) had known each other most of their lives. The Weikert and

Shriver farms were both located south of Gettysburg. George and Henrietta "Hettie" were married when George was eighteen and began their life together on the Shriver property. He had been responsible for operating the farm and the whiskey stills ever since his father had died two years before, when George was only sixteen. That responsibility had often been difficult for the young man. Maybe that was why he had become discontented.

Many evenings, after the children were asleep, he and Henrietta had discussed their future, sitting in the kitchen by the dim glow of candlelight. He knew he disliked the thought of being a farmer the rest of his life, so what could he do? They had come to the conclusion they would sell the farm when he was twenty-four and use the money to build a house in town. Once they had reached that decision, the next objective was to plan an income-producing business, but what? One blazingly hot day as he stood wiping his sweaty brow, it came to him. A saloon, that's the ticket, that's how I'll make money. Not only a saloon, but a ten pin alley. He had made a wild dash across the fields to tell Henrietta.

As Sadie hurried home, she remembered how Mama used to tell her why they had decided to move to town. She thought about the day they left the farm. It had been raining and everything seemed to go wrong. Because it was muddy, the wagon had slid down a gully, and Grandpa Weikert and Papa had to help the horses by pushing the wagon back on the road. And then the chickens had escaped from their coop, and everyone had to chase them and get them back. By this time all the grownups were drenched, exhausted, and coated with mud. But she and Mollie were nice and dry under the tarp on top of the wagon and watched with interest as the grownups started to laugh at each other. They were so covered with mud that the only thing you could see was the whites of their eyes. Everyone was relieved when they finally arrived at their new home.

Mama was busy making supper when Sadie arrived and Mollie was setting the table. Mr. Pittenturf was in the other room reading the paper and Lillie was asleep in her cradle.

"Guess what, Mama, our old house is empty. The people moved to Ohio."

"Well, isn't that something! They were there less than two years," said Mama. "In that case, I want you and Mollie to go in and see if everything I left in the garret is still there. Remember, when we moved to your grandparents', I had to leave everything stored in the garret. There wasn't any more room in the wagon. So, one of these days, you and Mollie go over there and take a look."

A week had passed and Sadie was anxious to see Tillie. Now she had an excuse. When Sadie and Mollie had finished their chores, they told Mama they were going to check the attic in their old house.

As they passed the Pierce house, they saw Tillie outside, and Sadie figured that Tillie would like to go with them. Tillie thought it was a capital idea.

"Do you think we should be scared?" Mollie looked a bit apprehensive.

"Of course not, silly. Mollie, stop being so dumb," said Sadie.

The three girls cautiously opened the unlocked door. The house smelled musty and dust covered the floors. They tiptoed up the stairs and climbed with trepidation to the garret door.

"What do you think will happen when we open the door?" whispered Mollie. "You know those soldiers died up here."

"Mollie, you know Mama just wants to know if her stuff is here. We'll take a quick look and then leave." Sadie swallowed and, pretending to be brave, carefully pressed on the latch.

Tillie was amused. "Look at you two. I'll go first in case there's danger," she said. Sadie and Mollie followed right behind her.

As they peered through the gloom, they could see several trunks, boxes, broken oil lamps, and a dilapidated trundle bed with frayed ropes. A mangy sofa with rips on the seat was in the far corner. They could see horsehair sticking straight up as though the sofa was scared of something seen or perhaps heard. On a nail hung several torn leather belts. In the corner were two wooden chairs, one with a missing back and the other tilted on its seat with two of its legs missing. Near the window, a dirty, bloodstained, grey hat caught their attention. There were other things too—dead flies, spider webs, and dust on everything.

"Looks like everything is still here," said Tillie. "But all this dust is making me sneeze, so let's go. You can come back another time and take some things you can carry back to your mama."

It sounded like a good idea to Sadie and Mollie although they were curious to see what was in the trunks and boxes.

That night, after they had gone to bed, Mollie whispered: "Sadie, what should we call Mr. Pittenturf? I don't want to call him 'Papa.' "

"I don't either," said Sadie. "Nothing sounds right, so I guess we can just keep calling him Mr. Pittenturf."

"How about 'Mr. P'?" Mollie giggled.

"For heaven's sake, Mollie, I don't think that would be proper," said Sadie with a snort, trying not to giggle. "I was just thinking about our real house," she said, soberly. "You were too young to remember when we moved there. You were only three. Listen, we moved on a miserable, rainy day. All our belongings were piled on two wagons with the chickens and us. Papa was so proud of the house he had built. He kept grinning at Mama and saying, 'Wait until you see it. You'll love it.'

"Don't you remember racing up the stairs to pick out our bedroom?"

Mollie shook her head. "Guess I was too young to remember very much. I'm sleepy, Sadie. I don't want to talk anymore."

Soon, both were asleep.

Chapter 2
New Neighbors

The next day Mollie promised to collect the eggs and let Sadie stay in bed for at least a little while. But that didn't happen. Mollie shattered the dream Sadie was having about Papa.

"Sadie, get up quick, we have new neighbors. Someone is moving into the house next door. That sure didn't take very long. The house was only for sale for a week," said Mollie, peering through the window. "Look, Sadie, there's a boy and a girl. Oh, let's go meet them."

"At least wait until I get dressed," grumbled Sadie. As soon as she had her clothes on, they hurried across the lawn and stood patiently waiting for their new neighbors to notice them.

Mollie whispered. "She's pretty and he looks like he would be fun."

The boy had been leaning over picking up a box when he happened to glance up and saw Sadie and Mollie. He was a tall, lanky boy with a shock of blond hair hanging over his forehead. He was dressed in a blue, homespun shirt and brown pants. His brown shoes were muddy.

"Hey, are you our new neighbors?" he called.

"No, you are OUR new neighbors," said Sadie grinning.

The boy grabbed his sister's hand and sauntered across the lawn. His sister was taller and more slender than Sadie. She had straight, brown hair worn quite short and was wearing a pale green dress with dark green trim. The two of them smiled.

"Hi, my name is Jason and this is my sister, Amy. We just moved from Baltimore. See all those boxes and baskets? Our parents are busy pushing the furniture around in the house and we have to carry everything else inside. What are your names?"

"I'm Sadie and this is my sister, Mollie. We can help you awhile, if you would like."

"Oh, I'm glad that you will be our neighbors. There weren't any girls in the neighborhood where we lived in Baltimore," said Amy with delight. "Thanks for your offer. We can sure use your help."

The four of them finished carrying everything inside in no time at all.

"I like them," said Mollie as they hurried home.

"Me too. Won't it be fun to have neighbors our age? Amy said she was twelve, and you know I'm almost twelve too, and Jason is fourteen. So, ha, you're the youngest! School will be over real soon and we can have lots of fun all summer long. Bet they would like us to show them around."

Chapter 3
Henrietta Remembers

Henrietta was tired. Taking care of the house and baby Lillie was a lot of work. Sadie and Mollie were already in bed, but she still had some mending to do. Lillie had finally fallen asleep and Henrietta was sitting in her favorite chair with the soft glow of the oil lamp on the table beside her. The chair was so comfortable that she closed her eyes and leaned back her head. She had noticed recently that her hair was turning quite grey. Well, I am thirty-one, she thought. A few grey hairs had become noticeable three years ago when she learned of George's death at Andersonville Prison in Georgia. How she still missed him. Her thoughts traveled back to the time when their lives had changed. She slept and in her dream she was walking through a mist. Fighting her way through the mist, she saw herself in their old home, and she was living once again her life as it had been...

Spring 1861

With the possibility of war on everyone's mind, the citizens of Gettysburg talked of nothing else. They would stop strangers in town and ask what they had heard. It seemed as though everyone believed there would be a war. Finally, with great anguish, President Lincoln declared war on April 12,

1861. Southern states, one after the other, had seceded from the nation. He called upon the Northern states to be strong and asked for seventy-five thousand volunteers. Men from Pennsylvania and the other states, thinking the war wouldn't last very long, perhaps only a few months, decided to sign up. Many of the young men in Adams County formed Company K and were mustered into Pennsylvania service on June 8. That day many Gettysburg folks gathered at the train station to see them off. They sang patriotic songs, waved flags and hugged the men, wishing them luck and praying for their safe return.

Henrietta, George, and the girls had also walked to the station. Mollie had not been feeling well, so Henrietta decided to take the girls home. George knew most of the men who were leaving and since his friend Jacob Hartzell was standing close by watching the men getting on the train, he told Henrietta he would stay a little longer. When the train left, George and Jacob slowly walked home. Neither of them wanted to talk, and all the other townspeople heading home were silent too.

So much was happening so quickly that it made George's head spin. He stopped and faced his friend. "I don't know, Jacob. I feel real bad about all our friends going off to war. Sure wish I knew what to do, but then how can I leave Henrietta, Sadie, and Mollie and go off to war? How could my wife take care of the business?"

Jacob shook his head despairingly. "Friend, you and I will just have to wait and see what happens. Maybe the war will be over real soon. Let's not worry yet."

The days became longer as spring turned into summer. The war news was so discouraging that George knew he would have to make a decision about doing his patriotic duty. How he hated the idea of leaving his family. Most nights he would stay awake agonizing about what to do. He would toss and turn and finally slip out of bed before dawn to think some more. Jacob had told him that some of the men he knew were joining Company C of Cole's Cavalry, and George had decided to do the same. And so one early morning as he hunkered down next to the woodpile on the porch, he knew what he had to do. He would join Cole's Cavalry with Jacob. But how was he going to tell Henrietta?

That evening after supper, George wanted to have a quiet time with her so he could tell her of his decision. He felt so many different emotions and knew it was going to be one of the most difficult tasks he had ever faced. Watching Henrietta bustle about the kitchen making supper, while Sadie set the table and Mollie sat in a corner quietly playing with her doll, kindled such love for them. He thought, how can I leave them? This is my family; how will they manage without me? Abruptly he rose from his chair and, feeling his stomach churning, he swallowed a sob. As Henrietta placed a tureen of soup on the table he attempted a smile and slowly embraced her.

When supper was over, George went out to the pump and filled two buckets with water. One was needed to wash dishes and the other for the kettle on the stove, kept warm for their bedtime ablutions.

Then it was Sadie and Mollie's bedtime. After a big hug and kiss for their mother, they followed George upstairs. Usually Henrietta tucked them into bed, but tonight George wanted to spend this time with his daughters. With the days becoming longer, he had been using the extra daylight working on outside chores, so this was a treat for all three. Little did the girls know how special this time would be for there wouldn't be many more days to spend with their papa.

Henrietta, while washing dishes, could occasionally hear the girls giggling and George's laughter as he told them their favorite story. It seemed to her that his laugh seemed forced. Then, it hit her like a thunderbolt! Of course! He had been talking to Jacob Hartzell, and she knew that he had made his decision. She heard him come down the stairs and slowly walk into the kitchen. Before he could say a word, she began to cry.

"George, you joined the cavalry and you're going off to war with Jacob. I hate this, all of this! Why do you have to fight?"

George held out his arms and she ran to him. He held her tightly.

"I must. It's the right decision, but oh, how I'll hate to leave you and the girls. Jacob and I signed up today with Captain Cole's Cavalry."

Tears streamed down Henrietta's face. She couldn't speak when George told her they only had twelve days together before he had to leave on September 9.

She nodded, feeling so helpless. There was nothing she could do to change what was happening.

The days seemed to fly by, each one bringing George's departure closer. Every day he chopped wood so that Henrietta would have a supply for winter. Sadie and Mollie helped stack the kindling into a neat pile. They tried so hard to be helpful, but they could only carry one piece at a time to the woodpile. At first they thought it was fun, but soon they became tired. George told them to go in and help their mama. He could actually do the job much quicker by himself, but he hadn't wanted to hurt their feelings. He had really enjoyed their help, knowing he would soon be leaving.

As long as Henrietta kept busy, she didn't have to think painful thoughts. What would happen when George was gone? Could she keep a bright smile for Sadie and Mollie? She sighed as she knitted socks for George. She had made several shirts, packed his shaving equipment, a plate, fork, knife, tin cup, and coffee, just in case. And of course his Bible.

Finally the day came. She had dashed to the hen house to collect the eggs just as the sun was rising. It was going to be a beautiful day. It should be a rainy, dismal day in keeping with how she felt, but she knew in her heart it was wrong to think that way. I should be grateful that the men have this day to travel to Frederick, Maryland, she thought. But please, Lord, keep George safe and well.

Rushing to the house, she called George, Sadie, and Mollie to hurry down for breakfast. So little time left. Jacob was coming before noon so he and George could leave together. She could hear George waking Sadie and Mollie and heard them laughing. They didn't understand that their papa was going away for a long time.

George had just come downstairs with them when Jacob arrived. "Howdy, Jacob, why so early? Thought you were coming at noontime. We haven't had breakfast yet."

"Morning, George. Well, I heard last evening that Captain Horner wants us to get there as soon as possible, so I figured while I'm in town, I'd let you know first and then go see some of my relatives to say goodbye. I'll be back in an hour."

"Oh no," Henrietta whispered, realizing she was wringing her hands and knew she needed to keep her emotions under control for the sake of the others. "Well, at least breakfast is ready, and, George, your knapsack is packed. Maybe Jacob will be a mite late, so let's sit down and eat and have this time together."

The final moments had arrived. George and Henrietta held each other as though they would never let go.

"Please be careful, my dear," murmured Henrietta. And then the tears began. She tried to smile bravely, but it was so difficult. When Sadie and Mollie saw their mama's tears and Papa looking so sad, they both began to weep.

"Please, Sadie, Mollie, don't cry. I want to see you smile. That's the way I want to remember you and Mama," he said soothingly.

Gulping back their tears, the girls tried to smile. Just then they saw Jacob walking down the street hastily eating a sausage. He had bought a bag of sausages for the journey, but, unfortunately, the bag had broken and the string of sausages was trailing behind him. As the Shrivers watched, three hungry, determined dogs, planning to share Jacob's breakfast, grabbed the sausages and promptly began to eat them. Jacob was so engrossed with his own sausage he hadn't noticed the dogs. It was such a hilarious scene that Sadie and Mollie forgot their tears and started laughing. Jacob looked just like the Pied Piper. And when he looked around and discovered his sausages missing, he had such a doleful look that even George and Henrietta had to grin. Three dogs, quite satisfied with their delicious meal, quickly disappeared down an alley.

After one last hug for each of his loved ones, George tossed his knapsack into Jacob's wagon. First, they had to pick up Jacob's brother so he'd be able to bring the wagon back to Gettysburg, and then they'd be on their way to Maryland. Slowly the horses began to trot down the road with George waving goodbye until he could no longer see Henrietta and the girls.

****

She awoke with a start when the baby started crying. Her mending had fallen on the floor and her neck was stiff. She looked around still dazed and realized that she was once again in her home on High Street and she wasn't married to George any longer. She was married to Daniel Pittenturf. She had an infant to take care of. And it was 1867. Slowly she climbed the stairs to bed.

Chapter 4
Letters Discovered in the Attic

Summer 1867

It was time, Sadie thought. She was curious about the trunks and boxes in the garret. What would she find? Mollie had finally finished her chores. Sadie decided to carry two more armfuls of wood into the kitchen, so Mama would have plenty of wood for cooking and baking. She thought about Amy and Jason. Maybe they could go along. Amy had become her best friend and often she and Amy would sit on the back steps and discuss what it would be like when they could wear their hair in a bun. That would mean they were surely grown up. Amy had told Sadie that her mother kept saying, "Amy, you want to grow up too fast. Enjoy what you do today." Sadie knew her mother felt the same way. But sometimes it was so hard to be told what to do all the time. If they were grownups, they could decide what to do themselves, she had said to Amy.

Mama had given them permission to leave, so she and Mollie hurried across the lawn. Amy was sitting on her front porch.

"Hi Amy," said Sadie as they approached. "We're going to check out our old attic. Can you come with us?" Sadie looked down and began twisting a button. "Do you think Jason would like to come with us? Does he miss his friends in Baltimore? Has he made any new friends here?"

"Why, Sadie, do you like my brother?"

Sadie blushed. "I think he's very nice." She became very busy smoothing her skirt. They heard the door slam and there was Jason.

"Hi Sadie, what are you and Mollie doing? Going somewhere?"

Before Sadie could say anything, Amy piped up. "They're going to their old house over on Baltimore Street. It's empty and their mother left some things in the attic. They want to know if we'd like to go with them."

"Now, that sounds like a good idea. Let's do it, Amy. Hold up a minute while I tell Mother where we'll be."

As they walked to the old house, Mollie kept up a commentary on the families that lived in every house they passed.

"Guess you and Sadie know almost everyone in town. Sure wasn't like that in Baltimore. Well, we knew some of our neighbors, but the city has lots more people than Gettysburg." Jason laughed. "I know I'll like living here, so I can know everyone just like you do."

When they climbed the stairs to the garret, Mollie trailed behind the other three. What would they find, not only in Mama's things but maybe there was something else. When she finally reached the attic door, she saw Sadie already opening a trunk.

"Oh, Mollie, look, Papa must have saved all our letters and given them to Mama the last time he was home. Look, here's my first letter to him. Remember when Tillie taught us to read and write? It was so exciting and I remember the first thing I wanted to do was write to Papa. Listen to this."

> *Dear Papa,*
>   *I can read and rite. Tillie teaches me. I can read to Mollie. I help Mama so does Mollie but I help the most. I miss you Papa and wish you were here. Mama hopes you won't get hurt or sick. Me too.*
>   *Your loving dowter*
>   *Sadie*

Jason was peering over her shoulder. He laughed. "How old were you? About eight?"

Amy nudged him. "Stop teasing Sadie. Just think, she can save the very first letter she ever wrote." She smiled at Sadie. "Bet you were around six when you wrote that."

Sadie nodded and carefully folded the letter and put it in the basket she had brought with her. She reached into the trunk and found some more letters carefully tied with a ribbon.

"Look, here's a letter from Papa, Mollie. Remember how we walked to the post office every day hoping to get a letter from him? Mama was always so disappointed when Mr. Buehler shook his head sadly and would tell Mama, not today. And when we did get a letter, we were all so excited. Mama was so happy to hear from him. Listen, I'll read it to you."

> *My Dear Beloved Wife and my Darling Sadie and Mollie,*
>   *I pray you are all well. I think of you often and wish I could be with you. We have returned to our*

camp at Harpers Ferry to have most of our horses shod that have been shoeless. We have been engaged in missions against General Mosby's Rangers and have captured many prisoners. Since I have left home, we have been in the saddle most of the time with no chance to write to my loved ones. But now I have an opportunity to have some free time. I climbed up to the top of the mountain overlooking Harpers Ferry, so I could be alone and think of you while I'm writing this letter. All of the men from Gettysburg here with me are courageous and in good health. If you see any of their families, please give them the news. I must close now. My courage does not falter and I pray that I will soon return to my loved ones.

　　Your Loving Husband, George

While Sadie read the letter out loud, the other three made themselves as comfortable as possible. Jason sat on the dirty floor with his back resting against a trunk. Amy and Mollie perched on top of another trunk. When Sadie had finished reading the letter, all of them were quiet. They were thinking about George being so far away and lonely.

"You're going to be really dirty, Jason," scolded Amy. "Mother won't be happy when she sees your trousers."

"I can wipe the dust off when we leave," answered Jason, "so don't worry. Sadie, that was some letter. Your father was a brave man. I've heard stories about General Mosby. The Confederates depended on him and his men to capture our men, destroy bridges, ambush trains or anything else they could do to cause trouble. He was a tough foe, but your father's cavalry must have been just as dangerous."

"Our papa was a very brave man. We all missed him so much since he wasn't able to get home very often," said Sadie pensively.

"Look, Sadie, here's a letter for you. See, 'Miss Sarah Shriver.' Who is it from?" Mollie held the letter out to Sadie. At the bottom of the letter was the name, "Captain John Pierce."

"Don't you remember him, Mollie? He was in charge of the Porter Guards from New York who stayed with us for several months in the winter of 1862."

She turned to Jason and Amy. "Guess Mollie was too young to remember. Some of the Porter Guards were quartered in the bowling alley out back and ate in the saloon in the cellar. Mama prepared their meals and the army paid for the food. I was sound asleep when they arrived and their voices woke me up, and then I smelled food. When I got downstairs, I bumped into a man in uniform. At first, I thought it was Papa. The man knelt down and smiled at me and told me his name was Pierce. Then Mama asked me to bring spoons down to the saloon. She had made potato soup, and since I was now wide awake, I could help her.

"It was lots of fun to have the soldiers here, and I especially liked Captain Pierce. I used to spend as much time with him as I could. He didn't mind because I reminded him of his daughter, who was the same age as I was.

"Mollie, remember how we used to walk to the Diamond in the evenings with Mama? The soldiers would parade around the Diamond to the music of fifes and drums. All the people would gather to watch them, and when they played patriotic songs, everyone joined in singing. And remember when it snowed and the soldiers had a snowball fight in the back-yard? Mama was laughing so hard she had tears in her eyes. Some of the soldiers grabbed Sergeant Walker's kepi and filled it with snow."

Sadie started to giggle and explained to Jason and Amy: "You see, he was practically bald and they jammed the kepi back on his head. Then Captain Pierce came outside and they really got him. They all started throwing snowballs at him, and one mighty icy ball knocked his hat into the snow. With one quick motion he scooped up his hat, dashed up the steps and rapped on the back door. Mama was still laughing when she opened the door. I'm glad we had some of the Porter Guards here. They stayed until temporary barracks were built outside of town. There were several places where the others were quartered. So they needed the barracks until they were ordered—I think—to Washington."

"What does the letter say?" asked Jason.

"Just that he was glad to have a chance to know Mama, Mollie, and me and that when the war was over, he would bring his daughter to Gettysburg to visit us," Sadie answered sadly. It was very special to get a letter from him. But I've never heard from him again. So I don't know what happened. I'm sure that if he were able to come or at least write another letter he would have done so. Guess I'll never know what happened to him."

Abruptly, she stood up. "It's getting late. Mollie and I had better go home before Mama worries about us. Let's plan to come back tomorrow afternoon. It's going to take awhile to look at everything."

They all stood up and Jason brushed off his trousers. "Hey Sadie, can we go to the cellar? I've never been in a saloon. I'd like to see what it's like."

"Sure," answered Mollie. "Come on, but we have to hurry."

As they scrambled down the stairs, Amy tapped Jason on the shoulder. "You'd better not have ever been in a saloon. Father would whip you without mercy if he found out."

"Never fear, dear sister, didn't you hear me say I'd never been in one? But that doesn't mean that someday when I'm much older, I wouldn't enjoy, ahem, a saloon." He winked at Amy.

Amy laughed. "Well, just don't tell anyone else that!"

The saloon looked just about the same as Sadie and Mollie remembered. The floor was brick, and the long wooden table and benches were still there.

"This is amazing," said Sadie. "It looks like the people who lived here for the last two years didn't remove anything. See the pewter tankards and even some clay pipes."

Jason was awed. "All this place needs is some men enjoying it."

The next morning, Amy ran over to see Sadie. Sadie was gathering eggs when she heard Amy call.

"I'm in the hen house," Sadie yelled.

Amy stood gingerly in the doorway. "Sadie, we can't go with you this afternoon. We have to go with our parents to visit relatives. Jason said to tell you that the next time you go, we can come along."

Sadie turned around with her basket of eggs and told Amy, "We'll wait until you can go. Today probably wouldn't be such a good day anyway since we have extra chores to do."

Chapter 5
More Finds in the Attic

Mollie came bouncing down the back steps. "Sadie, Mama said we don't have to hoe the garden today. She wants us to find something." She waited with anticipation to see what Sadie would say.

"What does that mean?" said Sadie crossly. "Something? Where?"

"Well, we have to go to our old house. Mama thinks the quilt she made for our bed is in one of the trunks in the attic. Remember, Grandma Weikert had lots of quilts, and I guess Mama decided that the quilt was one less thing we needed to pack." Mollie skipped along beside Sadie, but suddenly stopped. "You think we'll be all right? I mean just because it's the two of us?" she asked anxiously.

"Oh, Mollie, you're such a scaredy-cat. Don't be ridiculous. There's nothing there to be scared of. So we'll go, find the quilt, and then leave."

They were soon on their way. Everything in the garret looked the same. Same old dust, same dead flies, same spider webs. Sadie opened a different trunk. Inside they saw neatly folded articles of clothing and several quilts.

33

"That's the one we used to have on our bed, Mollie. Oh, it's so beautiful. And look, there's a couple of letters. Looks like one from Papa and one from Mama. Hold them and let's get going. I'll carry the quilt."

Suddenly they heard someone climbing the stairs. They stood frozen, listening intently and staring at each other.

"Sadie, Mollie, are you up there?" It was Tillie. With sighs of relieve the two girls ran down the stairs. Tillie was just ready to climb up the attic steps when she saw them.

"My goodness, you two are in a hurry. I thought I saw you go in the back door, so I figured I'd come to say hello. Oh, I see you have the quilt that had been on your bed, and I guess those are letters for your mother." The three of them sat on the steps.

Sadie nodded. "When we heard your footsteps, we wondered who it was. Glad it was you. It made me think about the time when your father came over all excited to tell us the Rebels were coming. Remember, Tillie? He insisted on us coming to your house while he tried to find out what was happening. And I remember Mollie and I crawled into your bed with you to keep warm, so it must have been winter. I tried to remember what you told us about the war but guess I was too young to really understand."

"Goodness, that was a while ago. Let me think for a minute. You're right to think it was wintertime. That happened in the winter of '61. And yes, my father hurried over, knocked on your door and insisted that you all should come to our house. There were always rumors that the Rebels were coming. My father hurried to the hardware store where everyone was talking about it. He finally came home after everyone realized it was just another rumor."

"I remember your mother was cross. She kept muttering, 'Those Rebels!' But what did we talk about when we were upstairs?"

"Well, Sadie, I do know you were frightened and wanted to know who the Rebels were. You knew that your papa was fighting them. And you were afraid they would come and hurt everyone. So I explained as best I could what the war was all about. I wasn't sure why the Rebels wanted to fight. But I thought it was because they believed in slavery, and President Lincoln believed slavery was wrong. Most everyone in the North wanted all the states to be one government, I suppose, but the Confederates believed they should be a separate government. They even elected their own president. That's why the war started. And I think I told you and Mollie not to be afraid even though I have to admit now I was also scared. I just didn't want you to know."

"Sometimes I think about the war. Some things I remember, and sometimes I don't want to remember. Guess I was too young to really know what it was all about. Yet now, I dream about the terrible things that happened," said Sadie forlornly.

"Just be glad the war is over. But I wish Papa hadn't died and we still lived here." Mollie wiped her tears away. She didn't want to cry.

Sadie patted Mollie's hand and then hugged Tillie. "We need to get home so we can give these letters to Mama. Come on, Mollie. Hope we can see you again soon, Tillie."

Sadie's face brightened as they ran home. "You know what we should do? Go on a picnic, and I'll ask Jason and Amy. We could walk out to Grandpa's farm and then go to Devil's Den. With all those huge boulders there, we can play hide and seek. That would be so much fun. And then maybe Grandpa would bring us home in his wagon."

Mollie jumped up. "That's an extra good idea, Sadie," she said excitedly. "We have to ask Mama right away."

Chapter 6
Letters and Memories

Henrietta, Sadie, and Mollie had stayed with Ma and Pa Weikert for almost a year after selling their home when the war was over. Henrietta missed seeing her parents every day now that once again she was living in Gettysburg. It had been hard work helping Pa with the plowing and harvesting but satisfying to work so hard that her muscles ached. She would be so tired at nighttime that she would fall asleep as soon as her head hit the pillow. It left little time to mourn.

Knowing she hadn't been able to keep her home and would have to sell it was difficult, but she had no choice. There was no money, and the only way to pay all the bills was to sell the house and also auction some of the furniture and household goods.

Now she was married to Mr. Daniel Pittenturf and they had an infant daughter together. Daniel knew what it was like to lose someone. His first wife had died a few months before George. His house wasn't large and beautiful like her beloved home with George, but it was adequate. There were two bedrooms, and Sadie and Mollie shared a room. Daniel had two sons from his first marriage but the youngest had died and the other son was living next door with his grandparents. Daniel, a

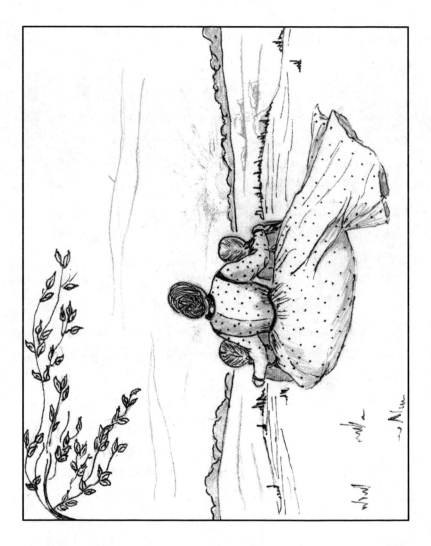

stone-mason and a blacksmith, was a kind man, but rather stern and reticent. The girls still didn't feel quite comfortable around him. Henrietta felt sure that would change when they realized what a kind man he was. It would just take some time.

She was tired. Washday was always a busy, tiring day—hauling in buckets of water to be heated on the stove, scrubbing clothes on a washboard, wringing them out and then hanging them on a clothesline. Sadie and Mollie would help hang the clothes and spread the small white linens on the grass to bleach in the sun.

Henrietta dropped into her favorite chair in the kitchen. It was a rocker her father had made as a wedding gift when she married George.

Yesterday, Mollie had handed her the letters they had found in the trunk and now she had time to read them. Opening the letter from George and seeing his familiar handwriting, she closed her eyes and began to rock. Thinking of him still made her want to weep. But she did want to read his letter. She opened her eyes and, holding the letter in trembling hands, began to read. She thought of George and how much she had loved him.

> *My Dear Wife,*
> *I can picture you and my darling girls right now sitting at the table while you read my letter to them. First, I want to congratulate you, Sadie. I received your letter and I enjoyed reading it first to myself and then to Private Hartzell and some of the other men. We all thought your writing was very good and I am very pleased to have your letter.*

It is very cold and windy and our tents aren't the best place to keep warm. We have a wood fire going constantly and when we're not out scouting for the Rebels, we hunker down as close as possible to the fire. A few days ago we captured some supplies and took four prisoners. Are you surprised to see on my letter that I am now a Corporal? Albert Hunter who used to live in Gettysburg has been selected 2nd Lieutenant of our Company and is very popular with our men.

The food is adequate but I surely miss your cooking. Jacob and I not only share a tent but take turns cooking. No doubt we are here for the winter. We drill four hours a day and are getting quite expert and the horses are being rapidly trained. In a few weeks we expect to receive our new uniforms and hopefully new tents as these are being torn up by the wind. Four Companies are quartered here. We did receive a new towel and a bar of soap and since our camp is supplied with hot water, we are at least clean for the present.

I think of you often and you are always in my heart. I pray that you are well. Sadie and Mollie, too. Life is very difficult, I know, but surely this will pass and we'll be together again.

Your Loving Husband, George

When she had finished his letter, she smoothed it and carefully folded it. Then she opened her letter to him.

My Dear Husband,
I was so delighted to receive your letter. Today was very cold and the ground was covered with ice. I hurried to the Post Office hoping for a letter from you. The reward for an embarrassing fall on the way was well worth my dignity being upset, for there

as I had prayed, was your letter. And to think of it, you are now a Corporal! George, I'm so proud of you and so are the girls. Captain Cole has certainly made an excellent choice in selecting you.

Sadie and Mollie were so excited to have a letter from you when I arrived home. Tillie had stayed with them and they were doing their lessons. I'm so pleased with their progress. Sadie has become quite a reader and often reads to Mollie. Tillie made tea for us and then we sat down while I read your letter to them. We're all so happy when we hear from you: it makes the whole day special and it seems as though you are with us. Oh, George, how I miss you. The girls miss you too, and every night before they sleep we have a special prayer that you will remain safe and well and will come back to us soon. We have had snow on the ground for a week and the roads are so mucky, it's difficult for the wagons to make their way along Baltimore Street. Several wagons have been mired in the snow and mud outside our house. I brought coffee out to the people in the wagons and they are always grateful.

I sent a package to you containing some warm socks, a warm shirt and some coffee. The Porter Guards are still quartered in the ten pin alley but I believe they will be leaving in two weeks. Mrs. Garlach heard they will be moving to the warehouse until the barracks are ready on the south edge of town. Captain Pierce has said the men will hate to leave here. Apparently the officers want to have several companies in one place. All the men have been very polite and most helpful. They have cleared our walk of snow and also the whole block. Anna Garlach enjoys helping me prepare supper for the men and helping to serve them. Since she is a young lady of sixteen, I think the men enjoy talking with her as well. We will miss having them here.

The weather is so dreary. I think of you being up in the mountains and how cold it must be. Spring will arrive in two months and hopefully will make it easier to bear. But every month that passes makes me miss you more. Hopefully the war will be over soon and you will come home to us. I pray every night for this.

With my love and prayers,
Your Loving Wife

She smiled, remembering how embarrassed she'd been when she slipped on the ice. Two of the Porter Guards had seen her fall and helped her to her feet. They were worried that she had been hurt. And she had told them, no, only shocked because it happened so suddenly.

Her thoughts turned to the present. Mollie had been so exuberant about Sadie's idea of a picnic. It would be good for them to take a day for just having fun. Since school was over, they had both helped every day with the chores, so she had given them permission to have a picnic. As soon as she had said they could go, they were out the door.

Sadie and Mollie had hurried across the lawn to invite Jason and Amy. Mama had said they could go the day after tomorrow. That gave them plenty of time to get ready. Sadie was delighted that their new neighbors thought a picnic would be loads of fun and were able to come.

The next morning Sadie woke up early. She shook Mollie until she finally awakened. "Come on, Mollie, hurry up and get dressed. Let's get our chores done as fast as we can, so we can get everything ready for the picnic."

"I'm getting up," grumbled Mollie. "Stop shaking me. Mama and I are going to bake cookies this morning and bake extra bread for sandwiches, so you'll have to do my chores." She grinned at Sadie with a very satisfied look. "Why are you so excited? Is it because Jason is coming with us?"

Sadie gave her a poke and ran from the room. "Never you mind," she yelled as she ran down the stairs.

Mama and Mollie were busy in the kitchen all morning. When Sadie was finished with her chores and Mollie's too, she burst into the kitchen. She had been planning what food they should bring. There was plenty of ham and cheese for the sandwiches. She ran downstairs to the cellar and picked up a jar of canned pickles and a jar of peaches that Mama had preserved last summer. "Hmm, what else do we need? I know, some hard boiled eggs and something to drink, but I have to remember we have to carry everything. Mr. Pierce has some canteens. We can borrow them to use for water," she muttered to herself.

That night after going to bed, she thought with satisfaction that everything was ready for tomorrow. It was going to be a really special day.

Chapter 7
Devil's Den and Little Round Top

It was a perfect day for a picnic—a glorious, sunny day with just enough breeze to cool them off while they were walking.

Jason was already on the porch when Sadie and Mollie arrived lugging several knapsacks. "Hi, Jason, where's Amy? Look, we've divided the food into four knapsacks so each of us only have to carry one," said Sadie. She set the bags on the porch.

The screen door slammed as Amy appeared. "Hi, Amy, you get to carry one of these knapsacks. If both of you are ready, let's get Tillie. She has canteens of water for us. Her father said we can use his canteens."

As they walked to Tillie's house, Sadie continued, "You haven't been to Devil's Den yet, but first we'll go to Little Round Top where we can have our picnic. Wait until you see where we're going. Did you know that the second day of the battle took place there? We were at Grandpa's farm and it was just awful. Tillie was with us. His farm is real close to Little Round Top."

"That must have been terrible to be so close to the fighting," Jason said. "I've read a lot about the war, especially

44

about the battle here in Gettysburg." He looked at Sadie with admiration. "You must have been very brave."

Sadie shook her head. "Not really. Mollie and I were really scared, and I don't want to remember everything that happened. But anyway, let's just have fun. And guess what? We can play hide and seek at Devil's Den. Wait until you see those gigantic boulders!"

After a three-mile walk, they finally arrived at the farm. Grandma Weikert was enjoying a cup of tea on the front porch when they arrived. "Well landsakes, Sadie, Mollie, and Tillie, what a surprise!" She gave each a big hug. "And who might these young'uns be? Come set a spell. That's a long walk for you in this heat. Here, I'll get some cider."

"Grandma, this is Jason and Amy. They moved next door and we are going to have a picnic on Little Round Top and then play hide and seek in Devil's Den. Do you think Grandpa can take us home in his wagon? And then you can come along and see Mama."

Mollie nudged Sadie and whispered, "You sound like Mrs. Garlach. Sometimes you talk too much."

Jason looked around. "Boy, this is a big farm. Amy and I were never on a farm before. We moved from Baltimore and always lived in the city, but I like living in Gettysburg."

Grandma grinned at Jason. "Well, young man, I'm glad you and your sister moved here. Nothing like fresh air. Now drink your cider. Do you have enough food for your picnic? Well, I guess so by the looks of those knapsacks. Run along now and have a good time. Stop back and I'll see if I can talk Grandpa into taking you home."

"Bet you can, Grandma," shouted Mollie from the front yard. She was already through the gate and starting up the path. The going was rough, struggling up the hill. They were tired, sweaty, and hungry by the time they reached the top of Little Round Top. All collapsed with a sigh of relief.

"I'm starved! Bet we're all hungry. Mollie, help me dole out the sandwiches, eggs, and pickles. We should save the peaches for later. Mama preserved them and they are really, really delicious." Soon they were busy eating and no one had time to talk. After the long walk and now feeling content, they wanted to relax in the sun for a while before scrambling down the steep hill to Devil's Den.

"I was just thinking of the last time we were here," said Tillie. "Remember? Your grandpa picked us up in his wagon. Let's see, there was the three of us, your mama and mine, Anna and Mrs. Garlach, and, of course, your grandparents." Tillie was sitting with her back against a rock, looking over the valley with Devil's Den in the distance.

"It was a beautiful day just like this, and we all enjoyed the opportunity to have a picnic," Tillie said slowly. "We never dreamed that right here, a year later, there would be a terrible battle that left so many men wounded or killed." She paused, sighed, and went on: "There is a feeling of such sorrow here, and I guess there always will be. People will come here for many years to remember those brave men."

Tillie shook her head, almost as though she could shake those dark thoughts away, and then smiled at Sadie. "Anyway,

we had finished lunch when Mr. Garlach arrived to take us home in his wagon."

"I remember, Tillie. I got to sit with Grandpa and help him drive the horses. It sure made me feel important." Mollie stood up and stretched.

"I remember too," said Sadie. "And Grandpa and Mr. Garlach sat over on those rocks, smoking their pipes. I always wondered what they were talking about so seriously. You were sitting nearby, Tillie. What were they saying?"

"They were talking about the war. We were here in the spring of 1862. You know, after the Porter Guards had gone. Well, back then the war was not going so good for us. They were wondering why the Confederates kept winning the battles. We had more men, more money, and more artillery. And they talked about General McClellan who didn't seem to be doing very much to win the war. Then they mentioned another general who was going to be in charge of the whole army. Let's see, what else? Oh, I know. They talked about President Lincoln losing his son. He was the same age as you are now, Sadie. How terrible to lose a son so young. They say Mrs. Lincoln was never quite the same afterwards. They also talked about the big battle between our USS *Monitor* and the Confederates' *Merrimac*. It was a draw, they decided, because both ships limped back to port. And I think that's about all they talked about."

Jason looked at Tillie with admiration. "How did you remember all that? My father used to discuss the war with our neighbors in Baltimore, but I don't remember very much of the war news. I read about it after it was over. Some of our neighbors favored the Confederates, and one of my best friends wasn't allowed to play with me because my parents supported the Union army."

"Don't forget, I was older than any of you, so I did follow the war news. And I have to admit I was eavesdropping. I figured they wouldn't appreciate my butting in while they were talking," Tillie said with a smile.

"Come on, let's go play. Last one to get to Devil's Den is 'it'." Mollie already had a head start when she hollered back to the rest of them.

"I don't want to be it," cried Sadie, and off she went, running down the hill.

"Me either," shouted Jason, bounding after her.

Both Amy and Tillie walked as sedately as possible down the hill. They were anxious not to fall or get their dresses dirty. By the time they reached the boulders they didn't see a soul.

"Tillie, we'll never find them," Amy wailed. "Look at all the places to hide."

"Don't worry, I know some good places where I bet we find them. Be quiet and we'll sneak up on them." Cautiously the two of them peered behind, in between, and on top of the boulders.

"There's Mollie," yelled Amy. "I see you on top of that boulder. Come help us find Jason and Sadie."

In the meantime Jason had found a great hiding place between two boulders. It was almost a cave. He crawled in

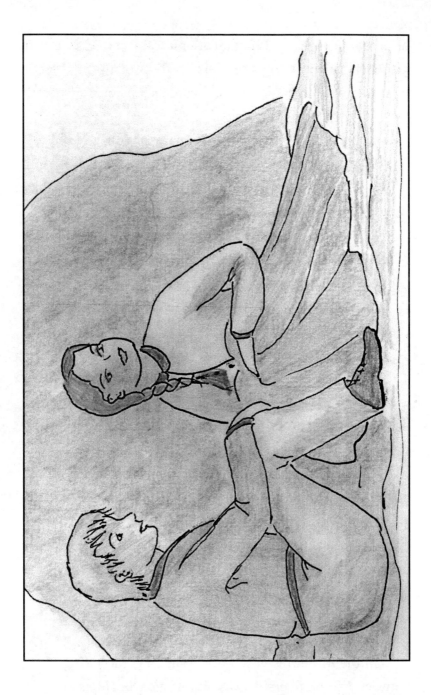

and figured they would have a hard time finding him. Hearing footsteps, he peered out and saw Sadie. "Psst! I'm in here," he whispered.

"Jason, that's where I was going to hide," she whispered back.

"Well, two of us can hide here. There's plenty of room, but be careful. Don't step on any loose stones that will rattle." Jason crawled farther into the crevice to make room for Sadie. The two of them were silent and listening intently. Suddenly they heard Amy yelling she had found Mollie.

Sadie leaned closer to Jason. "They can't see us in here." But being quiet was just too difficult for both of them and they started to whisper.

"This is a grand summer. I'm glad we moved next door to you, Sadie. When school starts, maybe we can walk together," he said shyly.

Sadie could feel her face getting red but fortunately their hiding place was dark, so Jason couldn't see her blushing. Suddenly Mollie's face appeared in the opening. She had tiptoed and they had been so engrossed they hadn't heard her. "I found them. Jason and Sadie are here," she shouted to Amy. "Come out you two."

Jason grinned at Sadie. "So much for finding a good place to hide. Go ahead and I'll follow you."

As soon as Sadie's head appeared, Mollie tagged her. "Now you're it, Sadie."

Jason crawled out and shouted: "Hey, Mollie, let's not play hide-and-seek anymore. Besides, this isn't the real way to play. I want to see how many boulders I can climb and explore."

Everyone agreed with his suggestion and they spent the rest of the afternoon exploring Devil's Den. It was getting late and finally time to leave.

As they trudged back to the Weikert farm, they were all thinking the same thing. Cool well water! It would taste so good. Grandpa Weikert was standing beside the well when they arrived. He had already filled the bucket and had the dipper ready. "Saw you coming down the hill and figured you'd be thirsty."

"Me first," yelled Mollie, grabbing the dipper.

"Well, the rest of us are polite and not grabby like you, Mollie. We'll take turns, and Amy and Jason can go first. I'll be the last one," Sadie said rather smugly.

Grandpa laughed. "Well, Sadie, that is being polite. When you all had your fill, come sit on the porch with me. I'll be taking you home, and Grandma is going with us. She still has things to do, so we may be sitting for a spell."

It felt good to sit on the porch and relax. "Now, Jason, I hear you and Amy came from Baltimore. I ain't never been there, but heard tell the Federal troops took over the city in the beginning of the war."

"Yes, we had soldiers there, and my father said it was like we were under siege. Some townspeople were arrested because they thought the South was right. I guess Maryland was really mixed up because some people favored the South and some favored the North. And since Baltimore is so close to Washington, the North wanted to make sure that the South couldn't attack the capital. Even churches had to fly the Union flag. He told me about the prison at Point Lookout."

Jason glanced at Sadie and Mollie. "We know how terrible Andersonville prison was, where so many Union soldiers died, but Point Lookout was just as bad. I remember my father saying there were twenty thousand prisoners there and four thousand died."

"Yep, guess both sides were pretty bad. No soldier wanted to be captured and taken to a prison." Grandpa was sitting in his favorite rocking chair and smoking his clay pipe.

"'Bout time you were ready," he grumbled as Grandma appeared on the porch carrying a basket.

Mollie lifted the cloth that covered the basket. "Sadie, look, Grandma has cookies and a cherry pie for us. Thanks, Grandma. I'll carry the basket for you."

Grandma laughed. "Guess I don't have to worry about losing that basket. Know you're going to keep your eyes on it, Mollie."

It had cooled off and they had a pleasant ride back to Gettysburg. Sadie sighed. She thought about all the fun they had playing hide-and-seek, especially when she and Jason were hiding together. The picnic had been a success, and it had been a most satisfying day.

Chapter 8

The Battle Had Arrived

Henrietta was again sitting in her rocker cradling Lillie after a tiring day. She smiled as she thought how excited the girls were when they returned from the picnic. She was so glad they had gone to Little Round Top and had such a good time. Maybe now their nightmares would stop. Suddenly she broke out in a cold sweat. She couldn't seem to move and closed her eyes. Nothing had been forgotten for her. She was living through the ordeal of war again. Everything was so clear; it seemed as though she was actually back in time. It was summer of the year 1863...

****

In January everyone was astir with the news that President Lincoln had issued the Emancipation Proclamation stating that slaves in the Confederate States would be free. It seemed that almost everyone at Gettysburg believed the president had done the right thing.

There hadn't been a day in the past year when there wasn't news about the war. Many people—both north and south—were discouraged and depressed. So many men had been killed or wounded in the prime of their lives. When would it stop? The North had lost two important battles—one at

Fredericksburg; the other at Chancellorsville. And now there were rumors again that the Rebs would be invading the North.

The townspeople were used to rumors. There had been stories in the past two years that the Rebs were going to attack, but nothing had happened. The citizens of Gettysburg were not lulled to complacency by these occasional rumors, for it was always possible.

It was a fine day in late June when the rumors became reality. Henrietta had been hoeing in the garden. Sadie and Mollie were helping by pulling weeds.

"The Rebs have come to town," shouted Mr. Pierce, as he came running up the street. He had been to the hardware store, and as soon as he heard the sound of rifles being discharged, he hastened home to tell his family and neighbors.

"Mrs. Shriver, you better get inside and lock the doors. They're shooting off their rifles to scare everyone and lord knows what else they'll do."

Henrietta only had to take one look at Mr. Pierce's face to know that this time it was really happening.

"Hurry, Sadie, take Mollie's hand and go in the house, NOW!"

Sadie grabbed Mollie's hand and dashed up the back steps and into the house. Without even thinking, Henrietta picked up the hoe and ran into the house and through the hall. She locked the front door, then rushed back to the kitchen to lock the back door. Sadie and Mollie hadn't moved.

"Hurry, we'll go to the cellar. We'll be safe there. If those Rebels try to get in here, I'm going to whack them with this hoe." It sounded quite brave and Sadie and Mollie must have believed it because they stopped trembling. They raced down the stairs and huddled together in the darkest far corner and waited—waited and waited! They could hear the rifles, men shouting, horses whinnying. What was happening? Henrietta wanted to distract the girls, maybe tell them a story, but fear silenced her. And so they remained quiet, listening intently to the frightening noises outside. Towards evening, there was a knock on the back door.

"It's me, Mrs. Shriver. You can open the door," a voice yelled.

Henrietta recognized Mr. Pierce's voice. Her legs were cramped and stiff but she managed to arouse Sadie and Mollie who had fallen asleep with their heads on her lap. She ran up the steps and with shaking hands, unlocked the door.

Mr. Pierce slipped inside. "I think it's safe to stay up here. The Rebs have gone but not before they did a lot of damage," he said bitterly. "They just went into stores and grabbed what they wanted. Got food, clothes, and even money. You should have seen them. What a ragtag bunch of men. They came riding into town, shot their rifles off to scare everyone, and then after they loaded up all they could take with them, they cut the telegraph wires. The bridge outside of town was destroyed, so now no trains can come here, no newspapers, either. Everyone is safe though; they didn't hurt anyone, as best we can tell. You three better get some dinner and go to bed early. It's been a mighty terrible day."

Henrietta clasped her hands tightly together. Now that the immediate danger was over, she began to shake. "Is your family all right? Did they stay in the cellar? Where are the Rebels now?"

"Well, I don't rightly know where they are, but they moved east. We saw them go. Sure hope they keep going and won't come back. The family's fine, a bit scared, but then I guess we all are. If you need anything, you just come over. I best be getting back so Mrs. Pierce won't get worried." Giving Sadie and Mollie a gentle pat on the head, he quietly closed the door. "Don't forget to lock this," they heard him say and then he was gone.

The town had been isolated from any news for four days. The tension was exhausting. No matter whom you talked to, no one knew what was going to happen next. On the fourth day, long lines of cavalry could be seen approaching from the south. Some of the boys in town had scurried off to see what was happening. The dust was so thick it was difficult to see what color uniform the men wore. As soon as they realized it was the Union army, they dashed back to town yelling through the streets, "It's our cavalry, General Buford's men. Hurry up, come and see. They're coming down Washington Street."

People from all over town hurried toward Washington Street to welcome the troops. The young ladies stood in groups and began singing patriotic songs. Some of the townspeople carried buckets of water and dippers, knowing the men were thirsty, and others stood silently with tears of relief. Henrietta had run out with a bucket of water while Sadie and Mollie carried dippers. They stood beside the street watching as the men marched through. Mr. Garlach was standing nearby and Henrietta heard him invite some of the soldiers to dinner. It was apparent they planned to camp there. Many troopers would stop, lean down from their horses, and accept a dipper of water. Henrietta could see how tired and dusty they were. "Much obliged, ma'am," were the words she heard over and over.

There were so many men and horses, thought Henrietta. Why, that measly bunch of Rebels won't be coming to town now that our brave soldiers are here. Little did she or any other person in town believe that the morning would bring with it the most devastating day they had ever known.

Some of the neighbors were standing on the corner and she saw the Pierce family talking with them. As Henrietta and the girls approached, Tillie saw them.

"Isn't it exciting, Mrs. Shriver? I got home from school and heard our soldiers were marching into town right behind our houses. I wanted to pick some flowers to give them but I was so excited, I forgot. My pa said there must be at least six thousand men."

Henrietta smiled and gently put her arm around Tillie. "I just hope all will be well with us," she said quietly. "Tell your ma that we're going back home. I don't want to disturb her conversation, and Sadie and Mollie need their supper."

She hadn't wanted to hear any news or talk to the neighbors. Somehow, if she didn't know anything, she could just pretend all this was a bad dream—no Rebels, no soldiers, no war, just a peaceful summer evening, and George would be in the garden waiting for her. She closed her eyes, feeling faint. Henrietta grasped Sadie and Mollie by the hand and hurried home.

Chapter 9
The Shrivers Leave Home

July 1, 1863

It was so still that morning that it seemed as though the earth was holding its breath. Henrietta hadn't been able to sleep. It was already so hot and the humidity was getting worse. As she stepped out on the back porch, she realized even the birds weren't singing. The silence was ominous. She shivered and knew instinctively that the day would be disastrous. Back inside, she ran up the stairs. She wanted the girls to get dressed. They would have to be prepared for anything this morning.

"Hurry, girls! Get dressed and come down for breakfast." Sadie and Mollie knew she really meant business. In a few moments they came scampering down the stairs. As they reached the bottom step, there was a loud and frightening noise. Henrietta came running in from the kitchen. "Oh my God, I think that's a cannon! Stay right there. Don't move. I'm going outside to find out."

As she opened the back door, she realized it wasn't just *one* cannon. Now there were great clouds of smoke, the roar of many cannons, and the pinging sound of rifles. All the noise was coming from Seminary Ridge, north and west of town.

"It's a battle! There is really fighting and men will get killed," Henrietta whispered to herself. She bit her lip so she wouldn't cry out. She hastened across the alley and over to Washington Street where more Union soldiers, wagons filled with supplies and artillery, were steadily passing by. The men's faces were grim and determined as they marched to battle.

Suddenly she remembered that Sadie and Mollie were waiting for her to come and make breakfast. As she got back home, Sadie opened the door.

"Mama, what's happening? What's all the noise? Are there more soldiers marching into town?"

"Yes, Sadie, many soldiers, and there's going to be a battle. We'll have a quick breakfast and then go see the Pierces." As she bustled about the kitchen preparing the food, she was thinking about what they should do. Should they stay in town and hopefully keep safe in the cellar, go to one of their neighbors, or go to her parents' farm? Maybe that was the wise decision to make. If they walked out to the farm they would be safer, since that was three miles to the south.

Glancing at the girls, she saw how frightened they looked. Mollie couldn't eat and sat there with tears running down her cheeks. And then she began to wail. "Mama, what's happening? Are the soldiers going to kill us?"

With that, Sadie began to cry. Henrietta rushed over to the table and gave them each a hug.

"No, my dears, they won't kill anyone who lives here and certainly not us, but I am afraid some of the soldiers will be killed because it's a battle and it could be very dangerous for us to stay here." That moment she knew her decision was made. They would go to her parents' farm.

"Come on, we'll run over to Tillie's house. I want to talk to her parents." She grabbed Mollie's hand. "Don't dawdle, Sadie," she said sharply, "We need to hurry. I need to talk to Mr. Pierce."

"There he is on the porch," cried Sadie as they scurried across the yards.

"Hurry, Mrs. Shriver, come inside!" Mr. Pierce opened the door and quickly closed it. He almost pushed them into kitchen chairs. Mrs. Pierce and Tillie were standing there looking so worried that Henrietta knew Mrs. Pierce had been pacing the floor. "What are we going to do? Isn't this horrible? I'm so scared, I just can't think."

Mr. Pierce put his arm around his wife and looked gravely at Henrietta. "Well, we have to do something. I've talked to some of the neighbors and they are planning to stay in their cellars. We should be safe in ours and we'll bring food, candles, and blankets." He turned to his wife. "Don't be scared, my dear. You can get food ready. And, Mrs. Shriver, you and the girls should stay with us. I don't like the idea of you three being alone. Can't tell what'll happen."

Henrietta shook her head and swallowed. "Oh, Mr. Pierce, I made a decision before we came here and I want to go to my parents' farm. Don't you think it will be safer there? And maybe Tillie should go with us. At least we'll be far enough away from what's happening here." She glanced at the girls. She didn't want to frighten them any more than they were already.

Mr. and Mrs. Pierce exchanged glances and Mrs. Pierce nodded.

"I think that's a good idea; you'll be safer out there. You, child, will go with Mrs. Shriver. I'll feel so much better if I know you're there, Tillie. You'd best get started before it gets any worse. And don't you worry. Your pa will make sure no Reb will hurt us!"

Solemnly the ladies clasped hands. By now it was early afternoon. Most of the Union troops had passed on the way to the fighting.

"We'll be on our way as soon as I lock the doors," said Henrietta. "I promise to take good care of Tillie."

"I'll come with you to make sure the house is locked up tight. Sure you're going to be all right?" Mr. Pierce asked anxiously.

Henrietta couldn't talk; she nodded, and so they began their treacherous journey. The houses they passed all seemed empty, and she realized that the families were already hiding in their cellars or had left town. It seemed so dreamlike to walk down the empty street yet hear the sounds of battle behind them. Holding on tightly to Sadie's and Mollie's hands, she walked as quickly as possible. As they passed Cemetery Hill, she saw soldiers placing cannons in position to be ready for the Rebels.

One of the men called out, "You'd better hurry. We expect the Rebels will be shoot'n this way any minute. You don't want to git shot."

Henrietta nodded and quickly hurried along. The road was in miserable condition with deep ruts from the wagons

and horses that had passed earlier. It made walking difficult. The noise from the shells and rifles and the smoke was getting worse every minute. Sadie's and Mollie's faces were streaked with tears, but now dust was added, and their dirty, forlorn faces made Henrietta want to cry too, but she knew she had to be brave for their sake, and Tillie's. They hurried along Taneytown Road, often having to wait on the side of the road as troops marched by.

One of the officers, seeing their distress, brought his horse to a halt. "Madam, I see that you and the children are having difficulty getting past the troops. See that farmhouse just down the road? Wait there. Wagons going in your direction stop there. I'm sure one of the drivers will help you. Are you going very far?"

"Oh, thank you, officer. The children are so tired and frightened. We're going to stay with my parents until the battle is over. They live a couple of miles down the road. Good luck to you and your men."

The officer doffed his hat and briskly caught up with his men. Henrietta could see many soldiers milling around the farmhouse and noticed some wagons being loaded. As they walked into the farmyard, one of the soldiers smiled at them.

"Looks to me, ma'am, that you could use some help. We'll be on our way shortly with this here wagon. You and the girls can ride along with us."

"That's very kind of you, thank you. We'll be most grateful for the ride, especially the girls. They're overwhelmed by all this and so hot and tired. I'll be glad to get to my parents' farm. It's right on this road, so we won't be any trouble to you."

Henrietta wiped her forehead and leaned down to wipe the girls' faces. Mollie was clinging to her skirt, and Sadie was watching with apprehension all the hustle and bustle of getting the wagon loaded. Her face was so pale she looked ill. What a horrifying experience for children so young, thought Henrietta, as she placed a hand on each small head. They were looking at her so beseechingly, as if she could make this nightmare go away. Tenderly she gave them a hug. "You must be brave. We'll do the best we can."

The wagon was now loaded and they managed to climb into the rear with the soldier's help. There was just enough room to sit down among all the boxes and equipment. Soldiers continued passing through and shouting as they headed towards town. The hollering helped the men keep a brave face, but the cheering would stop as they got closer. Henrietta could see wounded soldiers lying by the road. Others were tending to their wounds as best they could. The driver of the wagon turned around and spoke to her. "Don't you fret, madam, we'll be there soon enough; pardon all the jousting. This here road is full of ruts; can't help but make it bumpy. And never you mind about those wounded men. They'll be fixed up right as rain and be able to go on fighting and whip those Rebels," he said, trying to be encouraging.

Henrietta knew that this was only the beginning and there would be many more wounded before this battle was over. She was never so happy to see her parents' farm as she was that day. All four of them were hot and dusty. Sadie and Mollie were so tired they could barely climb the steps to the house. As devastating as the trip had been, Henrietta knew their ordeal was going to get much worse.

Her ma came flying out the front door and tried to hug all four at once. "I'm sure glad to see you. The terrible sounds coming from town had me so worried about you. The fighting must be horrible and we've been watching all the men marching towards town. Are the soldiers near your house, Hettie? We already have some wounded in the barn. Hurry, come in the house. We need your help. Thank God you're here. Becky and I have been bringing buckets of water from the pump and Pa has been putting firewood in the kitchen so we can bake plenty of bread."

As Ma talked, she was hustling them inside. "Set a spell. Here's some water and some fresh bread. Rest a while, then, Tillie, bring this bucket of water to the barn. One of the army surgeons out there needs it. Hettie, you can get all the linens from the blanket chest in my bedroom and start cutting them up for bandages. Sadie, you and Mollie just sit there and stay out of the way or take a nap on the settee in the parlor. Then you can help me in the kitchen. I'm going to make some good, healthy soup."

Just then Pa came in carrying an armful of firewood. "Thank God you're here, daughter. Understand there's already some shooting on our road closer to town."

"Oh Pa, it's been awful. We left town about one o'clock and brought Tillie with us. There was some shooting along the way and several wounded men lying beside the road. One poor soldier had been killed. The road is crowded with men. The Rebs are coming across the fields from Cashtown. By now there could be fighting right in the town streets. I thought if we came here we'd be safer, Pa."

"I sure hope so, Henrietta. Don't have time to think about it. Plenty to do. Did Ma tell you about the wounded men in the barn? Gotta git back there to help."

The evening passed quickly. Henrietta cut linens into strips while Sadie and Mollie folded them. Pa carried them to the barn to be used for bandages. It was arranged that the whole family would occupy the large bedroom in the front of the house. This was Ma and Pa's room and there was enough room for everyone to sleep on the floor. Every other room but the kitchen would be used for the wounded. That night every-one lay there, exhausted, wondering what the morning would bring.

Chapter 10
The Battle Rages On

July 2. 1863

The morning brought another hot and humid day, but women were still preparing food in the kitchen. As soon as the temperature in the wood stove was just right, they would start baking. The sweat rolled down their faces as they worked. Henrietta mopped her face with an old rag and called to Tillie who was coming down the stairs: "Tillie, come have breakfast and then take food to Sadie and Mollie. I don't want them coming downstairs unless it's absolutely necessary. My pa wants you to help bring water to the men outside. We've already taken care of the men here in the house. As soon as the bread is baking, I'll come help you, and so will my sister, Becky."

Henrietta had to shout over the sound of cannons. The noise was deafening and it felt like the very house foundation would collapse from the vibrations. Not only the house, but the very earth was trembling. The sound of cannons, the crack of rifles, the agonizing cries of the wounded, and the piercing screams of wounded horses, some still harnessed to wagons, gnawing at their wounds until they died, all blended into a cacophony of death.

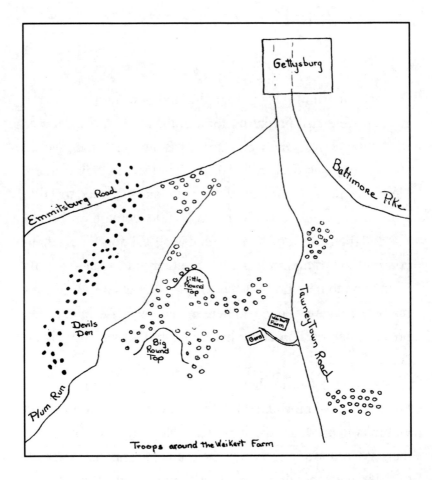

Gettysburg

Baltimore Pike

Emmitsburg Road

Taneytown Road

Little Round Top

Devils Den

Big Round Top

Weikert Farm

Barn

Plum Run

Troops around the Weikert Farm

A steady stream of wounded men was carried to the barn where exhausted surgeons valiantly operated on one man, then the next and the next and the next. Henrietta dashed across the lawn. She saw Becky and Tillie kneeling beside a wounded man. Becky was gently wiping the man's face with a wet cloth while Tillie was trying to place some water between his lips, hoping he could swallow. Henrietta grabbed a bucket of water and carefully stepped around the men who were lying on the grass. They had been carried from the barn after surgery. Some were moaning, yet there was a dull acceptance of pain, even death, revealed on their faces. She knelt beside man after man, trying to get each to drink some water and wiping the dust, sweat, and tears from each face, giving comfort as best she could. As she and the others were doing their best for these wounded men, the battle raged on with its noise, heat, blood, and countless more wounded and dying men. Wearily she stood up.

"Dear God, have mercy on these poor men," she murmured, clasping her hands together. Grimly she turned to help one more.

He was a young boy. Why, he couldn't be more than fifteen. She knelt beside him, his face so pale under the dirt and dust.

"What's your name?" she asked softly. "And how old are you?"

Weakly, he opened his eyes and with a voice so low she could barely hear him, he whispered, "Ma'am, Ah'm sixteen."

Gently she raised his head and helped him sip some water, then washed the grime and dust from his face. He was lying in the shade of the large oak tree near the porch. His leg had been amputated and a huge blood-soaked bandage covered the stump.

"What's your name? Where are you from?" She gently stroked his forehead.

"Ah'm from Tennessee, ma'am. Live with Ma and Pa." He looked at her and his face brightened. "Thank you, ma'am." She held his hand. "Will y'all write a letter for me? Tell 'em Ah won't be comin' home. Ah'm Willie Benson. Corporal knows where Ah live. See, he's over there, got his leg broke." He turned his head toward the fence. "Ah can see my leg over yonder on that pile of legs and arms." His eyes filled with tears. "Ma'am, will y'all make sure Ah have a coffin? Ah know there won't be enough to go around but Ah sure would appreciate it."

She smoothed the hair off his forehead. "Oh, Willie, of course I will, but you're not going to die. I promise to write to your ma and pa. I'll tell them how brave you are."

He closed his eyes and sighed. He seemed beyond his pain and she watched with anguish as he slowly gave up. His hand became limp and he was no longer breathing. Tears rolled down her cheeks as she gazed at this young boy who had died so far away from his loved ones and in so much pain.

She stumbled and slowly made her way between the wounded men, giving each a smile, wiping their faces and giving them sips of water. It seemed so little, such a small task in this living hell, but the men who lay there wounded or dying were grateful for her tender touch. It brought to them a sense of reality and reminded them of happy times with their loved ones, a precious moment when they forgot the tragedy of this day.

And so, all through this nightmarish day, Henrietta continued to do what she could for the poor wounded men. She could see the mounds of limbs piled by the picket fence growing and growing as the day dragged on. She was beginning to feel numb. She couldn't cry! Her grief and anger had to be controlled so she could continue to help. Would this day ever end? How could soldiers keep fighting?

The smoke from gunpowder, the dust, the stench from wounds, blood, and death combined with the heat was making it difficult to breathe. She suddenly realized that it was mid-afternoon and she hadn't had time to see to Sadie and Mollie. What would they be thinking? They must be absolutely terrified. She nodded to Tillie and motioned she was going to the house.

Her ma was in the kitchen packing bread into baskets. "I'm going upstairs to check on the girls," Henrietta shouted. Her ma nodded and continued with her packing. The sweat was rolling down both their faces and Henrietta knew it had to be overwhelmingly hot upstairs. But it was better to endure the heat than to see all the inhuman acts that men inflicted on each other.

Sadie and Mollie were crouched down in the far corner of the room. They leaned against each other and had clasped their hands around their knees, trying to become as small as possible. Their eyes were dull, almost vacant with shock, and tears had streaked their grimy, sweaty faces.

Henrietta knelt in front of them and hugged them. "It's all right, it's all right. Mama's here."

They clung to her but were unable to utter a word. They weren't able to express their fear and terror. Henrietta could feel their bodies relax as she held them. If only Ma or someone would come upstairs, she would ask them to bring some food and tea for the girls. Now was not the time to leave them.

Ma must have read her mind because she suddenly appeared in the doorway with some beans and molasses and hot tea on a tray. "I know they'd be needing this. You stay here, Hettie. No sense in going out to help the men right now. You stay with your girls and rest. Right now they need you. Later I'll come up and take your place and you can work in the kitchen. Already told Tillie and Becky we'll all take turns doing what's needed and always have someone stay with Sadie and Mollie."

The long, terrorizing, agonizing day at last came to an end. The thunder of battle had finally ceased but the moans and cries of the wounded continued. When the exhausted family settled down, they could hear the sounds of pain from other rooms, from the yard, even screams from the barn.

As darkness settled over the land, weary soldiers began to look for their wounded friends on the battlefield. Torches bobbed up Little Round Top as men stopped to peer down at bodies—some sprawled like marionettes, their limbs tangled in grotesque positions. The living were carried on stretchers to the barn where surgeons would struggle all night attempting what some might consider miracles. They tried stanching the flow of blood, probed for bullets, and faced the grim task of amputating one more limb of a barely conscious man—or boy. Those wounded soldiers who were past help were moved beside the piles of severed limbs to await death.

Chapter 11
The Last Battle

July 3, 1863

After a fitful night, Henrietta awoke to the sounds of muskets and cannons. The Union army feared that the Confederates would try to fight their way past Little Round Top and reach Taneytown Road, and so they had placed cannons on two sides of the house. Just as Henrietta stepped outside, an officer greeted her.

"Morning, ma'am. I just talked to your father and told him we have a carriage ready to take you someplace where you'll be safe. You can't stay here. Bullets and shells will likely hit the house. So please prepare to leave in a few minutes." He turned and rapidly went to the men who were ready for battle.

Henrietta raced inside to fetch Sadie and Mollie, calling out the news so everyone would be ready to leave. It didn't take the family and Tillie very long to run to the barn and pile into the carriage. The din of shells bursting, some directly overhead, was definitely a terrifying incentive.

Henrietta held on tightly to Sadie and Mollie as the horses raced down Taneytown Road. They finally arrived at a farm near the village of Two Taverns and found that other families had also fled to that area. Many of them lived on farms near the Weikerts, enduring the same dangers, and were overwhelmed by what was happening. The women and children gathered in the large farm kitchen where tea was being prepared. The men drifted out near the barn to talk about the battle and smoke their pipes.

Henrietta sat down close to Tillie and Becky, anxiously glancing across the room where Sadie and Mollie were huddling on the floor. Although her daughters were still not talking, they were sitting with a young girl about their age. Tentatively, the children began to play with the dolls the girl had brought with her.

"This will help them, I hope—doing something normal like playing with dolls. Maybe for awhile they'll forget this nightmare," Henrietta whispered to Becky, who nodded her head.

"Oh, I hope so, Hettie. In fact, I wish I was young enough to play with dolls myself." The two sisters clasped hands. Each understood how the other felt.

The afternoon dragged on and on. Everyone was restless and hot with little to do besides waiting and worrying. After what seemed more like days than hours, several of the women looked up, listening intently.

"I don't hear the cannons anymore," said one.

"No, it sounds like the fighting has stopped," said another.

Ma Weikert nodded her head emphatically. "I think it's time we head back home. Becky, go out and tell your pa to get the carriage ready. As soon as it's a mite cooler we're leaving. Hettie, be a good thing to wash the girls' faces and hands at the pump before we leave. Don't rightly know how much water we'll have at home, seeing as how we've been using so much yesterday and today, too."

The horses were soon hitched to the wagon, and Henrietta, her family, and Tillie started for the Weikert farm. Signs of the battle were everywhere. Along Taneytown Road, they saw broken fences, knapsacks, blankets, canteens, and other signs of battle strewn over the fields. Near the farm, they surveyed the horror of wounded men amongst the dead and dying, pitiful moaning and crying, and dead and dying horses. This was the aftermath of battle, thought Henrietta, not the glory of winning. No matter who won or lost, the result was the same for both sides: death and destruction.

She wanted so desperately to shield her daughters from seeing the terrible devastation. "Sadie and Mollie," she said firmly, "lie down in the wagon and don't move until I say you can." Hopefully they would miss most of the shocking sights.

They arrived at the Weikerts' and slowly proceeded to the house. They had to watch where they stepped because so many men were lying on the grass. When they walked into the house, they found many more wounded soldiers; in fact all the rooms were filled to capacity.

There was no time to rest. Everyone pitched in to help feed and care for the wounded. It was a long, long night. In the barn, the lanterns burned while the surgeons continued their ghastly task of removing bullets, bandaging wounds, and the worst of all, amputating limbs that were constantly added to the pile near the fence. Orderlies were digging a large trench so the limbs could be buried. Others were placing bodies in pine boxes and stacking them behind the barn.

Chapter 12
Returning Home

And now a new day! July 4th, a day for the whole nation to celebrate, or so it seemed. As everyone at the farm went about their tasks, they could hear the soldiers in blue cheering and knew that the Union army had won the battle. But they didn't have the energy or time to celebrate. There was too much to do. Doggedly, they continued their duties and hoped they could nurse these poor, broken bodies back to health.

For the next few days, a routine was established. The women who lived in Gettysburg took turns preparing food, feeding the soldiers and nursing them. The surgeons continued their grisly work. The men who could be moved were taken to churches and other large buildings in Gettysburg. Eventually, they would be taken by train to city hospitals.

Four days after the battle, Henrietta knew it was time to go home. Would her house still be there? What had happened in town? Soldiers had told the family that the Rebels had occupied the town since the first day. She hoped there was some food left and her vegetable garden was still there. But she knew that was highly unlikely. Thousands of soldiers had passed through the town, and with the battle taking place right there, nothing would be the same.

Once she had decided they must return home, Henrietta went upstairs to get the girls. As she trudged up the stairs, she glanced at her dress, which she had been wearing for seven days. It was covered with blood and dirt. When she got home, she was going to burn all the clothes that she and the girls had worn. She couldn't imagine keeping the clothes to remind them of these terrible days.

Sadie and Mollie looked up with blank faces as she walked into the room. They had been quietly listening to their grandmother tell them a funny story, but they were still unable to come out of their apathy. Henrietta would have been grateful for just one small giggle.

"We're going home, Sadie. You and Mollie run downstairs. Aunt Becky will give you something to eat before we leave. The fighting is over and we won't hear any more large booms. We'll be safe."

Sadie didn't say a word, but both she and Mollie hugged her and ran down the stairs.

"Well, Hettie, we still have loads of work to do but we can manage without you," said Ma. "'Tis best to git back home. Maybe the girls will be better because they're in their own home. Poor lil' young'uns. They don't understand why their world is all topsy-turvy. Now go on with you. Take care. Don't know when we'll git to town. Just glad you were with us, daughter. I'll say goodbye to your pa for you."

"Oh Ma, how can you always be so brave? You kept everyone so busy, we didn't have time to be scared. Hope you get a chance to rest soon. You and Pa need to take it easy."

The two hugged each other and soon Henrietta, Tillie, and the girls were on their way. It had rained and the road was so muddy they had to walk through the fields. The stench permeated everything. To draw a breath was nauseating, but Henrietta had prepared for this. She wrapped handkerchiefs soaked in peppermint oil around their heads to cover their noses. But what horrible sights…AGAIN…Dead horses with bloated stomachs still remained in the fields, along with ruined rifles, broken wagons, and army gear.

It was like walking through a nightmare, but it was real. There was a disturbing silence. All creatures had disappeared. The birds had ceased their joyful songs and the squirrels had stopped their chattering. All was still except for one sound—the buzzing of flies that covered the dead carcasses. Sadie and Mollie clutched their ma's skirt and never let go during that long silent journey. Henrietta and Tillie had no energy to speak to each other. They had withdrawn into their own thoughts. What will we find when we get home? Has the house been ruined by cannon balls? Will everyone be all right who stayed in town? Is there any food or water? Questions were running around in Henrietta's head like angry gnats.

As they got closer to town, they could see that nothing was the same. Trees looked forlorn, stripped of their leaves and most of their branches. Many of the houses had broken windows. Fences and gardens had disappeared. Evergreen Cemetery was in shambles with broken monuments scattered over the graves.

As they made their way up Baltimore Street, the first person they saw was Mrs. Garlach. She was hurrying toward them, red-faced and panting. "Landsakes, am I glad to see you. Tillie! Run along home. Your parents are fine but they're worried about you. I saw all of you dragging yourselves along and I had to come and walk you back home."

Tillie didn't wait to hear any more. With a nod she ran up the street.

"Now, Henrietta, I have to let you know what's been happening. First, the Rebels occupied the town for two and a-half days. They were right here after you left to go to your parents. What a sorry mess they left for us to clean up. And they ate all the food except what we could hide. And when the fightin' was over, they all had to drag themselves out of town. There was a long wagon train that left with all the wounded that could be moved. Then our men came back, but Henrietta, you should see all the wounded men. Why, they're everywhere. I have some, and Mrs. Pierce, too. In fact every-one in town is taking care of the wounded. And the men had to bury all those killed. Now they have to git to the horses, pile them up in big heaps and burn them. Why, there were close to five thousand dead horses around here, and we have about twenty thousand men here in town to take care of."

She paused for a second, wiped her sweaty brow with her apron, took a deep breath and put her arm around Henrietta. "So now, have to tell you the Rebels were in your house. They broke in your front door and were in the garret where they knocked out some of the bricks so they could shoot at our men on Cemetery Ridge. Well, two of them got themselves killed up there. Mr. Pierce saw them bringing the bodies out back."

Henrietta swayed and almost fainted. The very thought of Rebels in her house was unbearable. "Did they bury the bodies out back?" she asked with a shaky voice. "Did they take any of my things?"

"Henrietta, don't you worry. Those Rebels were taken away and buried, but I don't know if they took anything, but likely so. I heard they ransacked houses that were empty. But on the whole, they were decent to all of us in town. Kept telling everybody to stay in their cellars so they wouldn't get hurt."

They had reached Henrietta's house. The Rebels had smashed the lock, and the door was splintered, but at least it was closed. Henrietta pushed open the door.

"Well, would you look at that?" gasped Mrs. Garlach. They moved slowly down the front hall, glancing into the parlor and sitting room. There was a jumble of knickknacks and books; in fact everything had been taken out of drawers and shelves and now was scattered on the floor. Lamps and candlesticks were overturned and the drapes in the parlor had been torn down.

Henrietta felt her knees go weak as she slowly sat down on the stairs. It was just too much. She was so tired. The whole time at the farm, she had stopped herself from crying. But now the tears came. With her head on her knees and Sadie and Mollie beside her, she gave way to deep sobs.

"There, there," said Mrs. Garlach soothingly. "I know what you need to do first thing. Now you stay right there. I'm going to get a bucket of water and bring it upstairs and find clean clothes for the three of you. When you're clean, you'll feel much better. I'll go home and git a bite for you. Then you go to bed. Forgit everything. You three are plain tuckered out."

All Henrietta could do was nod in agreement. It wasn't long before Mrs. Garlach had everything ready for them. She had put fresh linens on the beds and found clean nightgowns. When the three had washed as well as possible, changed to fresh garments, and eaten the meal Mrs. Garlach had made for them, they crawled into bed and immediately fell asleep.

The next morning it was easier to face what had to be done. I'm going to burn those clothes and every article that was broken. And then put the rest where it belongs. I'll have to see about food as well, Henrietta thought. Since the girls were still sleeping, she decided to tackle the kitchen. It was a mess. Broken dishes, glassware, and garbage were strewn about. And two of the kitchen chairs were missing. She realized the Rebels had burned them in the woodstove. And there was nothing in the house to eat. She remembered Mrs. Garlach had mentioned the two commissaries in town where she could get food.

On July 11, trains were finally able to come to Gettysburg, bringing more food, medical supplies and volunteers. The townspeople would now have help with the wounded and cleaning up the town. The U.S. Commissary was established only a few blocks away where they distributed food and medical supplies.

After Henrietta restored some order in the kitchen, she woke the girls, and soon they were on their way to the commissary. There were many strangers in town. All seemed to have destinations in mind as they scurried along, trying not to breathe in the stench that permeated everything. Loved ones of wounded soldiers had come to help nurse them back to health. Henrietta and the girls hurried home, each carrying a basket of staples. It was such a relief to know that so many people were in town to help. Lord knows how we could have managed without these good people, thought Henrietta.

Each day the town looked more normal. Fences were being repaired and street debris was slowly disappearing. But the main, ongoing concern for everyone was caring for the poor, wretched wounded men and boys of both armies. Farm houses and barns, churches, public and private buildings and scores of in-town houses had, of necessity, become hospitals and, in too many cases, the death sites for hundreds of soldiers. Gradually, a huge tent hospital established just east of town began to fill with the seriously wounded, the dying, and some who were on the way to recovery.

Henrietta was busy helping the neighbors care for wounded men. She cooked meals and later provided sleeping accommodations for the relatives of the wounded. Both the Garlachs and the Pierces sheltered many wounded men, and it was a huge help to have Henrietta do all the cooking.

Many weeks after the battle, Mrs. Pierce and Henrietta had a chance to get together to enjoy a cup of tea.

"Oh, it feels good to relax. You know, Mrs. Pierce, the town almost looks normal again. If only we could get rid of the terrible smell, we'd all feel better. I've been so worried about Sadie and Mollie. They're still not acting the way they did before the battle. They're so listless and pale and hardly ever smile. I don't know what to do for them. And I'm worried about George. Haven't heard from him since June and it's now September. I know he would write if he could, so I must be patient and confident that I'll hear from him soon, but it's hard. It's such a letdown, Mrs. Pierce, going to the post office every day and coming home empty-handed."

Mrs. Pierce patted her hand. "Now, Henrietta, I know it's hard for you. Missing your husband and worrying about him and your young'uns is more than a body needs. But I do see Sadie and Mollie changing, slowly, mind you. I saw them playing in the leaves and even jumping rope on the back porch. They'll be all right. Just takes time. And you'll hear from George real soon." She nodded her head sagely. "He's been so busy chasing those Rebels he hasn't had a chance to write. I feel a letter is on the way. You'll be hearing from him this week, I truly believe."

Mrs. Pierce always made Henrietta feel better. She was so good-hearted and optimistic. Suddenly Henrietta did feel better. Maybe everything would turn around. She stood up, brushing her skirt.

"You're right. You always know what to say. I've already been to the post office, but who knows, tomorrow is another day, and maybe, just maybe, there'll be a letter."

"Wouldn't that be wonderful," said Mrs. Pierce. "Well, I must be going. Thanks for the tea. Oh, I almost forgot to tell you." She sat down again. "Mr. David Wills, and some other men have worked real hard to make the government put a cemetery here for the soldiers who died in battle. You've seen them working on it." She paused for effect. "They're going to have a big dedication ceremony in November. Why, Governor Curtin has been invited, and wouldn't it be something if President Lincoln would come? Now I'm going home," she said cheerfully as she stood up again.

"Well, that is exciting news. I'm glad there will be a national cemetery here. Can't think of a better place to have one. That would sure be exciting to see President Lincoln here in Gettysburg."

****

1867

Henrietta became conscious of tears rolling down her cheeks and feeling completely drained. Her reminiscences had been so real; as though she had actually relived those terrible days. She was shaking and carefully moved to the stove, heated some water, and fixed herself a cup of tea. Why do I have these awful flashbacks? Maybe so I can finally forget those terrible times, she thought. With slow and unsteady steps she walked upstairs to bed.

Chapter 13

A Summer Eve

One evening Sadie had a brilliant idea. At least she thought so. "Mollie, let's bring two kitchen chairs and the two oil lamps in the sitting room outside. We can sit on the back porch and watch the fireflies. Won't that be cozy? It'll be cooler out there since we had the rain shower this afternoon." She was thinking Jason and Amy would see them and come sit with them. Mollie fell into her plan without Sadie saying a thing about her thoughts.

As Mollie lugged out the chairs, she said, "Maybe Jason and Amy will see us and come join us."

"What a good idea, Mollie, maybe they will." Sadie smiled. The lamps gave a soft glow, and of course Jason and Amy would be able to see them sitting there, she hoped.

"What a good idea." Mama exclaimed. She stood by the back door fanning herself. "It's so cool out here."

Sadie got up. "Come on out, Mama, it's really nice out here. You can sit on my chair and I'll sit on the steps. Stop working and relax. I'll get some lemonade."

As they sat there enjoying the cool summer evening, they saw Jason and Amy walking across the lawn in their bare feet. Jason was carrying a small, brown paper bag.

"Guess what I have," he said as he sat down beside Sadie. "I remember you told us about Petey Winter's Sweet Shop, and since Amy and I walked down to Chambersburg Street, we decided to check it out. Boy, you were right; it sure smells good in there and there was lots of penny candy. And I remembered what kind you liked."

He held the paper bag out to Sadie. "I bought this for you," he said shyly. "There's plenty for Mollie and your mother, too. My father paid me to help him move some furniture. Amy got paid, too."

"You mean you bought my favorite, rock candy? Why, thank you, Jason." She grinned at him and her eyes sparkled. "Here, Mollie, have some. Mama, would you like some of my favorite candy?"

As they sat contently sucking on the candy and enjoying the cool evening, Jason turned to Sadie. "My father was saying that President Lincoln was here in Gettysburg dedicating the National Cemetery. Did you see him?"

"Yep, we did," said Mollie excitedly. "Tell him all about it, Mama. Sadie and I were too young to remember everything. I just remember there were lots and lots of people."

Mama laughed. "Yes, you were definitely too young to remember. After all, you were only six. Well, first of all, he came on the train from Washington the day before, and stayed at the David Wills House. There were so many important people in town that every hotel was filled. The next day the crowds were unbelievable. They walked up Baltimore Street and passed right in front of our house. We followed the crowd to the cemetery. Sadie and Mollie had the best view because Mr. Pierce and Mr. Garlach held them on their shoulders until Edward Everett started to speak and went on and on. As a matter of fact, he spoke for two hours. No wonder the men had to put you back on the ground. But then President Lincoln spoke. His speech only took a few minutes, but was interrupted by applause several times. When it was over, people clapped and clapped. When we were walking home, Mrs. Pierce said the president's speech was wonderful; that it was almost like poetry. I agreed. It was a beautiful speech. And you, young lady, yes, you, Mollie, cried out when he passed our house, 'Is that him in the big black hat? He's so tall and skinny.'"

"Mama, I was only little," said Mollie indignantly. "And he was tall. And he was skinny."

Everyone laughed. Jason stood up. "Golly, I wish I had seen him. Let's go visit the cemetery soon, Amy. We haven't been there yet. We won't see him but we can imagine what it was like when he gave his speech. Guess we'd better get home. It's getting late. Thanks for everything. This was fun, and guess I'll see you tomorrow. Come on, Amy. Good night, everyone."

"Well, let's bring everything inside." Mama opened the screen door.

"Mama, I think Jason likes Sadie. He bought her the kind of candy she likes." Mollie poked Sadie, as she said this.

"He was just being a good neighbor. Besides, you enjoyed the candy, too." Sadie poked her back.

Chapter 14
More Garret Surprises

Sadie and Mollie could hardly wait. They were going to the garret again, now that Jason and Amy could go with them. Sadie was anxious to see what else was up there. Eventually, when Grandpa wasn't busy, he was planning to bring his wagon to town, load up everything in the attic and take it to Mama. This might be the last chance to poke around.

Nothing had changed in the garret. Mollie wanted to look in the trunk they hadn't yet opened. As she rooted through the contents, she eagerly turned to Sadie.

"Look, Sadie, here's the dolls that Papa gave us for Christmas, the last time we saw him." Tears welled up in her eyes as she clutched her doll to her breast. "Why did Mama hide them up here?"

"Mama knew we'd play with them and probably get them dirty. This way, now that we're older, we won't ruin them and they'll always remind us of Papa."

Amy put her arm around Mollie. "Tell us about your papa. He must have come home to spend Christmas with you. When was that?"

Sadie answered. "Papa came home for Christmas after the battle in July… so that was in '63. I remember him riding

93

up the road on his horse. He looked so handsome in his uniform. I ran to meet him and he let me ride in front of him until we got here. Mama and Mollie were waiting for us, and I'll never forget how proud I was riding with him." She chuckled. "I was hoping all our neighbors would see me. Well, anyway, it was a wonderful Christmas. It had snowed and all the trees and everything were white. Mama had this wonderful dinner and Grandpa and Grandma and all our aunts and uncles came. When Mollie and I opened our gifts from Papa, I never expected to have such a beautiful doll. Mollie and I were so awed that Papa could choose them for us."

"Sounds like a real great Christmas," said Amy as she kneeled near the trunk. "Sadie, why was it the last time you saw him? What happened?"

"Papa had only a couple of days with us before he had to go back to Maryland. And on New Year's Day, he was captured by the Confederates and was taken to Andersonville Prison in Georgia. We never saw him again." Sadie's eyes glistened with unshed tears.

Jason had been leaning against a trunk while listening to Sadie, but he was restless and began to prowl around the attic. He didn't know what to say to Sadie and Mollie. He kneeled in front of the window and pretended to shoot towards Cemetery Hill. Looking down, he saw something wedged between the floor and the wall. "Look, here's a bullet near the window." He said excitedly, "This stain on the floor could be dried blood. Didn't you say some soldiers were killed here? And here's a bloody, grey kepi. Who were they?"

Sadie glared at him. "They were Rebel snipers. Don't you know that practically the whole town was in Confederate hands for almost three days? Everyone said that they were mostly polite to everybody who stayed in town, but they ransacked all the empty houses. Snipers got into our house because from here they could shoot at our soldiers on Cemetery Hill. And two of the Rebels were killed right here in the attic."

"Boy, it must have been really exciting to live here during the battle and see all the fighting," exclaimed Jason.

Sadie was so angry, she marched over to Jason and punched him on his arm, and then she punched him again. "How dare you say it was exciting! Don't you think about those dead soldiers and all the wounded? Come on, Mollie, let's go home."

She started down the stairs and Amy and Mollie followed her. Jason stood for a minute, thinking how ashamed he was to say the battle must have been exciting. Sadie and Mollie were very upset as they hurried home. Jason ran after them, saying, "I'm sorry, I'm sorry," but neither of them even turned around. Jason and Amy gloomily walked home.

"Jason, I know Sadie and Mollie were really upset, but tomorrow, why don't you go over and apologize. That will make you feel better and I'm sure they will understand," Amy encouraged him.

Sadie was still choked up when they arrived home. She had been sobbing so hard she could barely see. It was time to help with supper but she barely spoke to anyone. When finally all the chores were finished and Mollie had gone to bed, she sat in the kitchen with Mama.

"What's wrong, Sadie? I can tell you've been crying. You're pale, and your eyes are all red."

"Oh, Mama, we found the dolls that Papa had given us. You had wrapped them so carefully in an old tablecloth and Mollie wanted to know why you had put them away and I said it's because we would appreciate them now that we are older and can take care of them. And then Amy asked why that was the last time we saw Papa and I told her he was captured and died in prison. And then Jason said he thought the battle must have been exciting." Sadie burst into tears. "Mama, how could he say such things? What does *he* know? It was so awful, I'll never forget what happened. And then I punched him…twice."

Giving Sadie a hug and letting her talk was the best thing her mama could do. Sadie finally ran out of tears. "Go to bed now, Sadie. You're all tuckered out. Tomorrow you'll feel better."

It had been a tough day for the girls and Henrietta hoped they were sound asleep. Cautiously, she tiptoed up the stairs to check on them. Often Sadie had nightmares, but knowing how exhausting the day had been for her, Henrietta was pretty sure she would sleep well. After nursing the baby and making sure the older girls were asleep, Henrietta quietly closed the bedroom door and went downstairs.

Chapter 15
George Dies in Prison

In the kitchen Henrietta sat down in her rocker to rest. Today was three years to the day that George had died. She thought about the letter that she had received from a stranger— and remembered every word. It had been the worst day in her life to know that George was never coming home. Sadie and Mollie had been teary-eyed for days, and although she tried to comfort them, she was in deep mourning herself. Keeping the letter had been important, and every year at this time she read it again.

> *Dear Mrs. Shriver,*
> *I'm sending this letter to my relative in Adams County so he can mail it to you. I am a guard at Andersonville Prison and I knew your husband. He was a fine man and I regret to tell you, he passed away on August 25th, this year 1864. He asked me to let you know. Hoping this letter will give you solace by knowing what happened.*
> *Respectfully yours*

Henrietta sighed. Leaning back, she closed her eyes, re-membering the many horrible stories she had heard of Andersonville Prison. Once again, she couldn't move and broke out in a cold sweat. Suddenly she was in Andersonville Prison. Not only did she see George, she felt his suffering.

****

August 25, 1864

George opened his eyes and stared at the sky. The moon appeared from behind a cloud and cast its glow over the prison. It illuminated the stark outline of the stockade and the hundreds of men lying on the damp ground. He listened to the moans and coughing from the men nearby as they tried to keep warm by sleeping in spoon fashion. The night was chilly. It had rained earlier. Mosquitoes buzzed down to suck more blood from the bodies lying so close to each other. He was barely aware of their attacking him. He felt too weak to brush them away. Mosquito bites, lice, and gnats were only a minor irritation to the ill and dying men, as were the odor of unwashed bodies and the foul stench of open trenches filled with human excrement. Starvation and disease were the twin perils that crept closer and closer each day they were prisoners.

George tried to raise his head but it seemed like too much effort. His arm brushed the man's shoulder lying next to him and he knew the man had died. The body was cold. Eventually the guards would come and remove the bodies of those who had died during the night. They would be dumped into a mass grave.

He closed his eyes. Over and over and over in his mind, he had imagined the last few days he had spent with Henrietta and the girls. If he concentrated, he could feel the snowflakes on his face and hear the snow crunch as they walked to church. Or sitting side by side with Henrietta and seeing her sweet face; and seeing the delight on Sadie's and Mollie's faces as they opened their Christmas gifts. Was that years ago? He tried to think. No, it's August now, not even a year had passed. When he was captured, he remembered being in a different prison, but it all seemed so vague. He knew his friend Jacob wasn't here. Where was he? Was he captured too? He groaned. He was in such pain and it was difficult to move. He had lost so much weight that he knew he was slowly starving to death. His body had so little flesh on it that he looked like a skeleton as did the other prisoners. Sometimes he thought it would be easier to just let go and be at peace. No more hunger, no more pain. Death would be welcome.

What was it he needed to think about? It was important. The guard, yes the guard who had talked to him, had said he had relatives who lived near Gettysburg. He must find him. He frowned. He had to think, but it was so difficult to get his mind to work. I want to ask him if he would write to Henrietta when I die. That's it. He sighed and knew he was desperately ill. He would die here in prison just as the man beside him had died.

When dawn came, he would will himself to stand. I'll gather what strength I have and find that guard. I must do this. I won't die until I've found him. The moon had disappeared and he could see through half-opened eyes the beautiful streaks of color signaling a new day. Little by little, he managed to sit up. Gasping for breath, he sat with his head resting on his knees. The moans of the prisoners seemed louder as they faced another scorching day without shelter. There was movement, a head raised here, an arm there. The men knew there was another day to endure.

Using all the strength he had, George was finally able to stand. He swayed and almost fell. One step at a time, he thought. I WILL make it. Tottering like an old man, he began the longest journey of his life. I've got to get to the stockade over there. That's where the guard will be. Stumbling slowly between the other men, he managed to walk a few paces. Can't sit down, won't get up...rest a minute, then keep going, he told himself. It seemed like an eternity before he managed to get close to the stockade. Could he find the guard? Would he be there? Standing there and gasping for breath, he slowly looked around. Yes, there he was talking to another guard. Seeing the guard gave him a sudden burst of energy. Only a few more paces. I can do it.

The guard looked around. He realized a prisoner was walking towards him; a gaunt, emaciated skeleton with a long, ragged beard. The only part of the man that seemed to be alive was his eyes that burned with such intensity. Uneasily he watched this apparition approach, and suddenly he recognized the man. He was the prisoner from Gettysburg. And now standing in front of the guard, the prisoner put his hands out beseechingly.

"Help," he croaked, even surprising himself at the sound of his voice. His mouth was so dry, and not having spoken to anyone for days, he hadn't realized how he sounded. Talking to the other prisoners had been too much effort. He tried once more.

"Need...help, please." The guard knew this man was dying. He reached him and gently held him up, looking at his face. "Please...tell your relatives...near Gettysburg...find...my wife. Henrietta Shriver...on Baltimore Street. Please! Want her to...know...I...died." Each word spoken came so slowly and with so much difficulty, he could say no more.

"Yes," said the guard kindly. "I remember you and enjoyed talking with you about the apple orchards and farms where you live. It's my uncle who lives there and I promise to write him and let him know."

It was all George could wish for. His mission was accomplished. His eyesight began to dim. No longer could he see the guard who was holding him. His eyes glazed over and his body became limp. The guard carefully laid him on the ground. "He's dead," he said to the other guard. "He was dying before he even spoke," he said in amazement.

****

For a moment, Henrietta didn't know where she was. She was exhausted, but now she felt cleansed. She had lived through the tragedies of the past and could put them to rest. From now on, she would be able to only think of the good memories. There was going to be a future, maybe with problems, but she could handle them, and she had a new baby daughter to care for and watch grow up. She thought about what her mother had said after George had died. "Now, Hettie, I'm saying this for your own good. Life looks pretty bleak right now, but it will get better. You're still a young woman and I know you won't like what I'm about to say because you're still mourning, but I suspect some good man will want to marry you."

Her mother had been right. She was so very fond of Daniel and was happy to be married to him and felt blessed to have baby Lillie.

The girls were beginning to accept Daniel Pittenturf. No, he wasn't their papa like he was Lillie's, but he was a kind and thoughtful man and maybe now they might begin to call him "Father." Soon school would start and she was glad the girls had become good friends with the neighbors, Amy and Jason. They were so much happier.

Feeling so much lighter in spirit, she smiled as she climbed the stairs.

Chapter 16

Summer Is Over

Sadie was sitting on the back steps, thinking about everything that had happened this summer. If it hadn't been for Jason and Amy, it wouldn't have been as much fun. She was looking forward to school. Mama had made new dresses for her and Mollie and she planned to wear hers the first day of school and wondered if Jason would notice. Well, at least they were still friends. He had apologized to her for what he had said in the garret. She grinned. He had also said she had a mean punch!

She heard someone whistling and, looking up, saw Jason walking across the lawn. She got up and slowly went to meet him. After all, she didn't want him to think she was anxious to see him. Were girls supposed to be coy? She wasn't sure. She'd have to ask Tillie.

"Hi, Sadie. I saw you sitting on the steps. Amy is busy helping our mother and guess Mollie is helping your mama. So, uh, I was wondering, uh, well, would you go walking with me?"

"Yes." Sadie smiled.

Epilogue

The family left Gettysburg in the 1870s. Sadly, Sadie's and Mollie's lives ended young. Sadie died from consumption just before her nineteenth birthday. Mollie married but bore no children and succumbed to consumption before turning twenty-three. Henrietta, who was often called Hettie, lived to be eighty years old. Baby Lillie grew up, married, and produced three grandchildren for Hettie, the eldest named Henrietta Pearl. George Shriver left no descendants.

Throughout the 1900s, the Shriver house, located at 309 Baltimore Street in Gettysburg, Pennsylvania, began to deteriorate and was nearly condemned. However, in 1996, a restoration project was begun, and the house is now a museum, open to the public. Visit the Shrivers' old home and imagine George, Henrietta, Sadie, and Mollie living there. Or take a virtual tour at www.shriverhouse.org. Their neighbor's house, Tillie Pierce's homestead, located at 301 Baltimore Street, also still stands and is operating today as a bed and breakfast. Learn more about Tillie and her house at www.tilliepiercehouse.com.

George W. Shriver

In the midst of preparing to open Shriver's Saloon & Ten-Pin Alley, George mustered into Cole's Cavalry. Two years later he was captured at Rectorville, Virginia, and imprisoned at Andersonville.

Courtesy Shriver House Museum and
Anne and Dan Nemeth-Barath
(photographers)

Henrietta "Hettie" Weikert Shriver

During the Battle of Gettysburg, Hettie took her two daughters to seek safety at her parents' farm. The Weikert farm sits between Big and Little Round Tops.

Courtesy Shriver House Museum and
Anne and Dan Nemeth-Barath
(photographers)

Sadie and Mollie Shriver

Daughters of George and Henrietta "Hettie" Shriver. During the Battle of Gettysburg, Sadie (7) and Mollie (5) left their home with their mother to take refuge at the Weikert farm at the base of the Round Tops.

Courtesy Shriver House Museum and Anne and Dan Nemeth-Barath (photographers)

Confederates Occupy the Shriver House

During the Battle of Gettysburg, Confederates seized the Shriver family home. At least two soldiers died in the sharpshooters' nest they had set up in the garret.

Courtesy Shriver House Museum and R. J. Gibson (photographer)

Shriver House Museum

The home of George, Hettie and their daughters, Sadie and Mollie, was built in 1860. Today guided tours through all four floors of the house tell the civilian side of the Battle of Gettysburg.

Courtesy Shriver House Museum and Donny Thompson (photographer)

Confederate Sharpshooters' Nest

During the Battle of Gettysburg, Confederates seized the home of the Shriver family and set up a sharpshooters' nest in the garret. Live ammunition, medical supplies, and bloodstains were discovered during the restoration—more than 133 years after the battle.

Courtesy Shriver House Museum and Linda Baker (photographer)

Shriver House Parlor

In 1860 George and Hettie Shriver built their spacious, new home in Gettysburg. The parlor was reserved for entertaining guests, holiday celebrations, funerals, and other special occasions.

Courtesy Shriver House Museum and Donny Thompson (photographer)

Shriver House Kitchen

The Shrivers' kitchen was located inside their home rather than in a separate building behind the house, as was customary.

Courtesy Shriver House Museum and Donny Thompson (photographer)

Sadie and Mollie's Bedroom

Children typically shared a bedroom in the mid-nineteenth century. Sadie and Mollie's bedroom displays typical items of the period: dolls, rolling hoop, Noah's Ark, ten-pin bowling set, slate board, and a chamber pot.

Courtesy Shriver House Museum and Donny Thompson (photographer)

Shriver's Saloon

Built in 1860, just months before the start of the Civil War, Shriver's
Saloon was situated in the cellar of George and Henrietta's new home on
south Baltimore hill.

Courtesy Shriver House Museum and Donny Thompson (photographer)

Educational Resources

Shriver Family History and Timeline

George Shriver was born on July 27, 1836. Henrietta "Hettie" Weikert was born on March 7, 1836. George and Henrietta were almost nineteen years old when they were married on January 23, 1855. Sarah Louisa, known as Sadie, was born November 21, 1855, and Mary Margaret, known as Mollie, on August 13, 1857. On June 4, 1859, a son named Jacob Emanuel was also born to George and Hettie, living only two months and twenty-four days. He passed away on August 28, 1859. George bought the property on Baltimore Street in May 1860.

The Civil War began in April 1861. Sadie was five and Mollie was three when the war began. George Shriver enlisted in September 1861 as part of Company C of Cole's Cavalry. The Battle of Gettysburg began on July 1, 1863. Henrietta and the girls fled town to the Weikert farm, located between Big Round Top and Little Round Top, where the heart of the fighting would soon be. Henrietta and the girls

114

returned home on July 7. George came home for Christmas that year, returning to battle on December 29, 1863. On January 1, 1864, he was captured while fighting in Virginia and taken to Andersonville Prison in Georgia where he died on August 25, 1864.

George's death left Henrietta a widow at the age of twenty-eight. She was married again to Daniel Free Pittenturf two years later on July 19, 1866. A widower with two small sons, Frank and James, Daniel had lost his first wife, Cynthia Powers, in April 1864. James died in an accident with scalding water shortly after Hettie and Daniel were married. Frank then went to live with his maternal grandparents, who resided next door.

Lillie Pittenturf was born on April 17, 1867. A second daughter named Emma was born to Henrietta and Daniel in September 1869. Emma died a month later. Sadie died on November 6, 1874. Mollie married William E. Stallsmith, a carpenter from Littlestown, Pennsylvania, on December 1, 1878. Mollie died on July 16, 1880. All three girls are buried in Evergreen Cemetery in Gettysburg.

Lillie married William Allen Hollebaugh on July 12, 1885, and resided in Annapolis, Maryland, for many years. They had three children: Henrietta Pearl, called Pearl; Ruby L.; and William Allen, Jr., called Billy.

After leaving Gettysburg in the 1870s, Daniel died in 1900 at the age of 71. Henrietta died in April 1916 at the age of 80 and is buried with Daniel and alongside their daughter, Lillie, in Washington, DC.

The Gettysburg Campaign

The Gettysburg Campaign was a series of skirmishes and one major battle fought over a three-week period in June and July 1863 when Confederate General Robert E. Lee attacked Pennsylvania.

Lee had many reasons for the attack: to move fighting out of war-torn Virginia; to capture a major Northern capital at Harrisburg; to take over the railroads there as a means of attacking Philadelphia, Baltimore, and Washington from the North; to shut down the Union's largest army training camp at Harrisburg; to close the coal mines in northeastern Pennsylvania, thus eliminating a major source of energy for Northern factories and the Union navy; and to rally a peace movement in the North.

Lee's Army of Northern Virginia had moved up through the Shenandoah Valley of Virginia into the Cumberland Valley of Pennsylvania during the last week of June. On June 30, Confederate cavalry under Brigadier General Albert G. Jenkins raided Mechanicsburg and skirmished with Union troops at what is now Camp Hill, three miles west of Harrisburg.

At the same time, Major General James Ewell Brown "Jeb" Stuart, chief of Lee's cavalry forces, led his troopers around the Union army, skirmished with Union cavalry at Hanover, and burned the army post at Carlisle before riding south to Gettysburg.

When the fighting near Gettysburg broke out early on July 1, Lee recalled his cavalrymen and began to mass his army west of the town. The Battle of Gettysburg (July 1 through July 3) was the greatest and largest battle ever fought in the Western Hemisphere and is generally considered the turning point of the Civil War. Major General George G. Meade's Army of the Potomac defeated Lee's army in this three-day battle fought by 160,000 soldiers. In both armies, more than 7,000 men died, some 33,000 were wounded, and almost 11,000 were reported missing.

One day after the battle ended, and in a driving rainstorm, Lee's army retreated back down the Cumberland Valley. While the army struggled almost fifty miles on their anguished trip to the Potomac River at Williamsport, Maryland, a wagon train seventeen miles long carried an estimated 11,500 wounded Confederate soldiers down a separate route to Williamsport. Due to flooding and destruction of their temporary bridge, Lee's army was forced to set up a defensive position with their back to the river, awaiting attack by Meade's army.

Almost ten days had passed since the Battle of Gettysburg ended. But just hours before Meade was set to hit the trapped Confederates, Lee's army managed to get across the Potomac to the safety of Virginia. The Gettysburg Campaign had ended.

Information on the Town of Gettysburg

At the time of the Civil War, approximately twenty-four hundred citizens lived in Gettysburg, a busy and interesting town. It was the county seat, and a college and a seminary were located there. Picture a hub of a wheel and the hub is Gettysburg. The spokes are all the roads that led to and from the town. There were many inns where travelers could stay.

Farmers made up the rest of the population in the county and would come into town for supplies.

Research and Discussion Questions

The American Civil War

What were the economic differences between the North and the South? Why did these differences exist?

What were some of the other differences besides economics between the North and the South? Why did the South want to secede from the Union and start its own government?

How did the Civil War start and where?

Why was the state of Maryland so important to the North?

What was the Underground Railroad? Find out how it operated.

During the Civil War there were prisons for captured soldiers in the North and South. What were the conditions in these prisons? How did they differ from prisons today?

The Battle of Gettysburg

Learn as much as you can about the Battle of Gettysburg.

How did the Confederate occupation of Gettysburg for two and a half days affect its citizens? How did they survive?

While the Confederate troops invaded and occupied the town of Gettysburg during the war, they did not intend to hurt or kill the town citizens or civilians of Gettysburg. How do their actions and intentions compare with later wars or wars and conflicts of today?

How did the citizens of Gettysburg react to the wounded and dead soldiers? Find out how many soldiers were wounded and how many died during these days of battle.

How many Gettysburg residents were killed during the battle?

What problems had to be taken care of after the battle?

Medicine in the Civil War

During the war, many soldiers were injured or had one or more limbs amputated. Find out about the primitive procedures used during an operation.

Sadly, Sadie and Mollie Shriver both died at a young age from the disease *consumption*, which today is called *tuberculosis*. How was that illness treated in the 1800s? How is it treated today? What are the symptoms?

Henrietta lost two children in infancy, a son born to George in 1859 who lived less than three months, and a second daughter born in 1869 to Daniel who lived only one month. What were the infant mortality rates during the 1850s and 1860s? What kind of health care was available to infants and children as well as pregnant women and women during childbirth?

Living during Civil War Times

Sadie, Mollie, Amy, and Jason were intrigued to spend their summer exploring the old attic. Find out about the type of toys and games available during those years. Are there any that we still have today?

Today we have many conveniences such as cars, electricity, television, computers, and washers and dryers. What conveniences

Troops move into Gettysburg
Drawing by the author's grandson, Logan Cook, age 13

did citizens in a small town have in the 1860s? Imagine your-self as a teenager living back then. What would your life be like? What would you do during a typical day without the luxuries you now enjoy?

The Shriver family home housed the family and George's business, Shrivers' Saloon and Ten Pin Alley, a bowling alley that was inhabited by Union soldiers in the winter of 1862. When was the game of bowling invented and how did it dif-fer from the current game and bowling alleys today? What other sports were played in the Civil War era?

At the urging of her family, Henrietta marries Mr. Pittenturf who becomes the girls' stepfather. Find out why economic and social conditions for women made it almost necessary for Henrietta to remarry so quickly. Could Henrietta have gotten a job to support herself and the girls?

The People during the Civil War

The Shrivers' neighbors' daughter Tillie Pierce accompanied the Shriver girls to the Weikert farm during the battle at Gettysburg. Find out more about Tillie's life and writings.

Much of what we know today about the Civil War has come from personal letters, diaries, and memoirs from the soldiers and civilians. Research other first-hand accounts of the battle. How are they similar to the story of the Shriver family? How are they different?

Suggested Further Reading

At Gettysburg, Or What a Girl Saw and Heard of the Battle: A True Narrative by Mrs. Tillie Pierce Alleman. West Lake Borland, NY, 1889.

Crossroads of Gettysburg by Alan N. Kay. White Mane Kids, Shippensburg, PA, 2005.

Days of Darkness: The Gettysburg Civilians by William G. Williams. White Mane Publishing Co., Inc., Shippensburg, PA, 1986.

The Shrivers' Story: Eyewitnesses to the Battle of Gettysburg. Shriver House Museum, 2008.

Window of Time by Karen Weinberg. White Mane Kids, Shippensburg, PA, 1991.

Young Heroes of Gettysburg by William Thomas Venner. White Mane Kids, Shippensburg, PA, 2000.

About the Author

KAJSA C. COOK, a former school-teacher, is a graduate of Pennsylvania State University. She has served as one of the first tour guides for the Shriver Museum in Gettysburg and is active in the Adams County Arts Council. A resident of Gettysburg, she has three sons and seven grandchildren.

WHITE MANE PUBLISHING CO., INC.

To Request a Catalog Please Write to:
WHITE MANE PUBLISHING COMPANY, INC.
P.O. Box 708 • Shippensburg, PA 17257
e-mail: marketing@whitemane.com

CPSIA information can be obtained at www.ICGtesting.com
Printed in the USA
BVOW02s0305200314

348242BV00005B/6/P